ANGIE SPADY

with Channing Everidge

PUBLISHING GROUP
Nashville, Tennessee

Also in the Desperate Diva Diaries series:

Catie Conrad: Faith, Friendship, and Fashion Disasters

Published by B&H Publishing Group

Printed in the United States of America

ISBN: 978-1-4336-8461-6

Dewey Decimal Number: JF

Subject Heading: GIRLS—FICTION \ POPULARITY—FICTION \ FAITH—FICTION

1 2 3 4 5 6 7 8 • 19 18 17 16 15

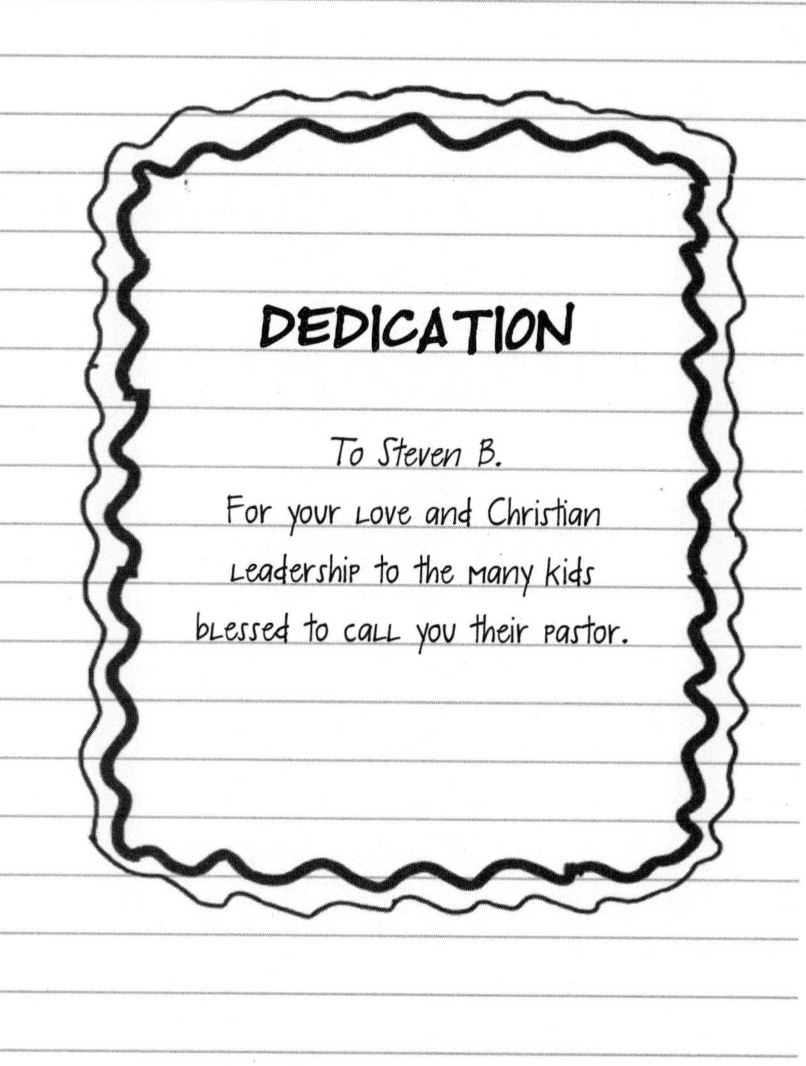

DEDICATION

To Steven B.

For your love and Christian leadership to the many kids blessed to call you their pastor.

So here I go, another diary to fill up!

FRIDAY, JANUARY 17

I CANNOT believe that I've already filled up an entire diary and I'm starting on the second!

WEIRD.

If anyone had ever told me (*especially DAD*) that I'd write my most PRIVATE secrets in a crazy diary, I'd think that:

A. They'd totally lost it.

B. Their elevator didn't go all the way to the top.

C. They must have me mixed up with some kind of brainiac kid.

D. All of the above.

But Dad was right. This diary thing is kinda cool—ESPECIALLY when I've had a horrible day at school . . . *LIKE TODAY.*

Or when I need to come home, forget about Miranda Maroni, and just design stuff in my sketchbook . . . *LIKE TODAY.*

It all started in P.E. class. . . .

Did I mention that I do NOT like P.E.? Well, I DON'T, and neither does my best friend, Sophie Martin. Maybe it's because Coach Calloway treats us like we're in the Army. One minute he's saying "drop and give me twenty-five push-ups!" and the next he's yelling "the next kid who complains is going to do a thousand laps around the gym!" Well, maybe he didn't say **1,000** laps, but it was something like that. I wouldn't be surprised if he blows that whistle one of these days and makes us scrub the toilets with a toothbrush.

But today it wasn't Coach Calloway who put me in a bad mood—it was Miranda.

OF COURSE.

Miranda Maroni is the one girl in sixth grade who knows exactly how to get on my LAST NERVE. ☹ Whether it's rolling her eyes when I wear one of my fashions to school or her NONSTOP bragging about "the latest accessory to die for," she drives me INSANE!

But today Miranda wasn't driving me crazy—she was being a total pain to Sophie. ☹

I guess I should mention that Sophie is captain of the middle school academic team. And if you ask me, the Clairemont Crusaders are LUCKY to have her.

GO CRUSADERS!

She not only scores more points than anyone else, she's also the smartest and most organized girl I know. *The exact OPPOSITE of me.* ☹ I can't remember the dates of boring old wars (why do we need to know that kind of stuff anyway?), and I can barely remember to study for those crazy algebra quizzes. (Who on earth needs to know the value of X+Y?!)

But Sophie never forgets a single thing. She even messages me at home to remind me of our homework assignments. THANK YOU, SOPHIE!

But after Coach Calloway made us sprint up and down the gym today (I almost passed out twice ☹), Sophie decided to get out her study questions and prepare for the next academic match.

Naturally, since I'm her BFF, I offered to quiz her until the bell rang. Sophie recited names of classical music composers one minute, and then she rattled off science definitions word for word! I don't know how that girl does it.

And for some reason that makes NO SENSE to me, Miranda decided to be her typical bully self. "Why are you wasting your time on that stupid academic team, Sophie?" she asked. "Talk about BOR-ING! Why don't you forget about that junk and try out for the volleyball team instead? We actually WIN games!"

UGH.

Yeah, she actually said that. Of course I shouldn't be surprised. She's Miranda Maroni: the RUDEST girl in class. ☹

You could have heard a pin drop in the gym after Miranda blurted out her two cents. I was almost sure that my mouth dropped open. Everyone in class waited to see what Sophie would say back to her.

"Whatever, Miranda," Sophie said. "Thanks, but I'll stick with the academic team. Good luck on your volleyball match against the Lions, though."

HUH?? I couldn't believe it. Sophie was actually NICE to her.

I don't know if I could have acted like Sophie. I'd want to say, "Thanks but NO THANKS, Miranda! Why would I want to be on a volleyball team with YOU? I'm WAY smarter than you'll ever be!"

But I'd only say that in my head. Even though I sometimes totally stink at it, I try to remind myself of **Psalm 34:13 (NIV)**: "Keep your tongue from evil and your lips from telling lies."

So yeah, I try to keep my mouth shut. But it's SO HARD with M.M.!!!

I practically pray for her every week since she drives me bonkers on a daily basis. Of course, I pray for myself, too, since I need a double dose of patience with her. Scratch that—TRIPLE DOSE!

Sophie and I were never so glad to leave P.E. class today. Once again, Miranda and Coach Calloway had ruined a perfectly good morning. . . .

I could hardly wait to get home and vent about it in my diary. At least I can write down my feelings and talk to God about it. Of course, I can also get my mind off things by drawing in my sketchbook. ☺

After all, the world's next

FASHION DESIGNER TO THE 

has to practice, practice, practice!

GTG!

There are some GORGEOUS dress designs in my future!!!!

← Rhinestones!

Purple leather!

NEW FALL RUNWAY COLLECTION!

SUNDAY, JANUARY 19

UGH. ☹

So much for sleeping late this morning.

The Germ and his RIDICULOUS pet skunk, Rosey, are driving me crazy!

As long as my little brother walks around carrying that furry little freak in his arms, he'll be "the Germ" and NOT Jeremy Conrad to me. "Jeremy" is way too normal a name for him.

What kind of kid hangs out with a skunk anyway? I'll tell you what kind—the same kind of kid who's convinced he'll have his own TV show on Animal Planet. Like I said: **RIDICULOUS!**

YEAH, RIGHT!

And this morning, the Germ REALLY pushed it.

I was sound asleep in my bed and having the most amazing dream ever: I was in Paris modeling the latest Catie Conrad Original—a floor-length blue gown with rhinestones and lace down the sleeves. IT WAS GORGEOUS, even if it was just a dream. To give it that extra touch of ooh la la, the dress had fur trim along the neckline. I posed for the cameras and signed auto-graphs for all the fans. It seemed JUST LIKE it was really happening!

That is, until I realized that it was NOT the fur on the dress that felt so soft. It was Rosey, or should I say, Rosey's TAIL . . . for **REAL!**

TALK ABOUT A NIGHTMARE!!!

That goofy skunk had been asleep in my bed and had her tail right ACROSS MY FACE! I'll probably need counseling until I'm fifty just to get over it.

"That does it, Germ!" I couldn't help it—I yelled. "Can't you keep that thing on a leash? It better stay out of my room OR ELSE!"

"Or else WHAT?" he smarted back, sticking out his tongue like a brat.

"Or else I'm gonna—" But then Mom interrupted me.

"Or else you BOTH are going to get grounded with no TV for a week. Or Jeremy, maybe you'd like to clean your sister's room, and Catie, you can clean Jeremy's?"

Yikes.

I know when to be quiet. There was NO WAY I was going to risk getting grounded by Mom. The thought of cleaning the Germ's room (including Rosey's Place, as my brother likes to call her skunk house) makes my skin crawl. And there's no way I'd let him get NEAR my sewing machine! He'd tear it up in two seconds, not to mention trample all over my fashion sketches with his big feet.

Of course, the Germ is always trying to make excuses for Rosey being a **TOTAL PEST.**

Who knows how long that creature had been lying in my bed with its tail across my face! I immediately ran to the bathroom and scrubbed my face a zillion times. I used soap, shampoo, bath gel, and zit cream—all at the same time—just to make sure there was NO TRACE of that stink bomb on my skin.

The last thing I want to do today is to go to church smelling like a skunk!

GROSS!! GROSS!! GROSS!!! ☹☹☹

At least I'll have a row of seats to myself, since I'm sure no one will want to sit by me. ☹

Not even Sophie. Hopefully she'll be at church today and in a better mood.

Even though she didn't let it show, Sophie messaged me last night and admitted that she was hurt over what Miranda had said to her in P.E.

That made two of us.

Sophie: I still can't believe that M.M. said that 2 me on Friday. ☹

Catie: Don't let it get to U, Soph. She's just jealous.

Sophie: MayB. But it was SUPER HARD to act like it didn't bug me. God gave me strength. Do U think that being on the academic team is stupid? BE HONEST.

Catie: Who cares what ANYONE thinks! And it's NOT stupid! You guys are the SMART ones! Just forget about her. C U at church!

GTG!!!

Church was awesome today for SOOOOO many reasons:

1. I didn't smell like Rosey, and so Sophie sat with me. It could be because I spritzed myself from head to toe with Sweet Sugar body spray. (I now smelled like a birthday cake on steroids.)

2. Josh Henderson, aka the cutest boy in our class, came to church today and said "Hi" to me! He. Spoke. To. Me. . . . **AND SMILED!**

3. Our youth pastor said it was okay, sometimes, to be frustrated with God when we talk to Him. He said David was sort of angry with God when he didn't understand why things happened, but God is patient and listens. I felt A LOT better after hearing that. I'd been pretty upset with God on Friday when Miranda was so rude to Sophie.

But when Mom said we needed to run an errand after church, my whole day went from **BAD** to **WORSE!** Right now, I can't even talk about it!!!!

MONDAY, JANUARY 20

Okay, so I've calmed down a little. It's taken me 24 whole hours to talk about it, but here goes:

After church yesterday, Mom promised the Germ that we'd stop at the Crafty Corner to pick out **VALENTINE CARDS** for his class.

Yeah, it's ALREADY that time of the year. ☹

I guess I shouldn't have been surprised since the Crafty Corner puts out their Christmas decorations in July.

However, I'd rather not think about the most embarrassing holiday in the history of EMBARRASSING holidays!

UGH. UGH. UGH. UGH.

Some of the girls in class **LOVE** Valentine's Day.

NOT ME. ☹

AND NOT SOPHIE. ☹

We're not ready to have real boyfriends yet. You know, not really. I mean, it's not like I'm old enough to get married or anything—even if it were to be to Josh Henderson, the cutest boy ever.

But try telling that to Miranda Maroni. She has a NEW crush on a NEW boy EVERY MONTH!

Oh, and today she VOLUNTEERED to help Mrs. Gibson with the Valentine's Day bulletin board.

Of course she did.

But here's the thing: Miranda NEVER volunteers for anything, so I knew she was up to something. I think she did it to drop hints to the guys.

As soon as she stapled the last heart to the bulletin board, she waltzed into class and said, "Wow! Valentine's Day is just a FEW WEEKS away! I sure hope I get some yummy chocolates, or better yet, ROSES! Or if someone REALLY wants to be nice, they'll get BOTH! That would be so awesome—don't you think, Emily? Emily? Don't you think so?"

Blah . . . Blah . . . Blah . . .

Miranda said it loud enough to wake the dead. And her sidekick, Emily, is always around to back up anything she has to say. I'm sure Miranda will force her to carry all the roses, cards, and chocolates she'll get from every boy on the planet.

UGH.

But what will Sophie and I get?

ZERO.

ZILCH.

GOOSE EGG.

IT WILL BE SOOOOOO EMBARRASSING!

Of course, our homeroom teacher will give every kid a piece of candy that's so hard it could BREAK A TOOTH. She'll say, "All of you hold a special place in my heart," and I'll pray I don't end up at the dentist office.

Sometimes Dad sends me a single rose with a card that says, "You'll always be my little sweetheart."

BUT. THAT. IS. NOT. THE. SAME. My parents DO NOT UNDERSTAND things like this.

When I reminded Sophie about Valentine's Day this morning, she acted like it was no big deal.

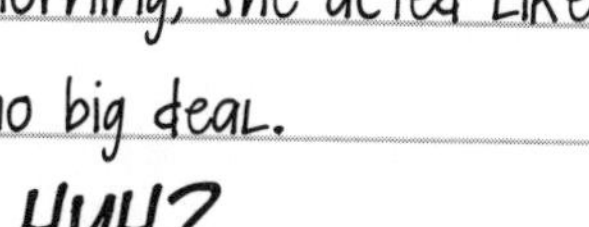

HUH?

HUH? HUH? HUH? HUH?

Catie, you're freaking out over nothing! It's just a goofy made up holiday! Go draw a dress or something!

Who are you, and what have you done with my best friend Sophie?

This was NOT the same Sophie that had been my best friend since second grade. She usually dreaded Valentine's Day as much as I did.

She didn't even seem upset with Miranda anymore.

WHAT'S GOTTEN INTO HER???

I, on the other hand, had a hard time forgetting what Miranda had said to my BFF last week. Miranda Maroni could be such a **SNOB**!

I am so glad that this day is finally O-V-E-R!!!!

I guess it's time to add M.M. to my Prayer List . . .

ONE. MORE. TIME. ☹

1. Learn to forgive snobs like M.M.
2. Quit worrying about Valentine's Day!!

TUESDAY, JANUARY 21

I could SO tell that Sophie was stressed out today.

She was **ONE. BIG. NERVE.**

But I understood. After all, Saturday's academic team match against Whitman Middle School is one of the biggest matches of the entire year—AND a qualifier for district competition!

According to Sophie, Whitman has a guy on their team who acts like a human calculator. At the last match, when the judge gave this kid fifteen seconds to solve a graph problem, he did it in five. And when his team was given two-step equations to solve, Sophie said he didn't even write them down—he just did them in his head in ONE STEP.

WHOA.

I wouldn't even ATTEMPT to do such a thing. I STINK at math.

But I'm not sure why Sophie was freaking out about it. She did the same kind of thing in math class today. When Mrs. Marlow asked us to solve −24 + −49, Sophie did it in her head and blurted out the answer like it was nothing.

And just when Sophie proved why she had the highest grade in math, I noticed something out of the corner of my eye. Although Sophie didn't notice it, I saw Miranda look over at Emily and roll her eyes when Mrs. Marlow said, *"Excellent job, Sophie!"*

GRRR . . . SO TYPICAL MIRANDA. She couldn't stand it if someone was better at something than her. I gave Miranda "the look," just so she'd know that I saw her. Why did she have to be so jealous?

I'm sure Miranda REALLY FREAKED when one of the guys said, *"Wow, Sophie is such a brain"* after Sophie finished her worksheet way before everyone else.

I'm shocked that Miranda's eyes didn't roll back into her head! LOL!

LOL!

If only I could be as smart as Sophie. If I had just HALF the brain she does, I'd be happy.

The other kids on the academic team are brainiacs too. It figures! ☹

Lauren Webb takes piano lessons after school, so I'm sure she knows everything there is to know about Mozart or Bach. Sometimes I hear her practicing in the band room after school.

She's incredible. Sophie says Lauren's been playing since she was four years old. I don't know how her hands fly all over that keyboard so quickly, but it always sounds beautiful. I can barely play "Mary Had a Little Lamb." ☹

Ian Kendrick has the highest grade of anyone in English class. Every single time I see him, he's got his nose stuck in a book. One minute he's reading *The 39 Clues*, and the next he's reading *Harry Potter* for the zillionth time. He probably has every page memorized.

And Zoey Franklin is ALMOST as smart as Sophie. She knows more random facts than Wikipedia. Her parents probably let her spend ALL the time she wants on the computer.

NOT ME.

No wonder they're all on the academic team—EVERYTHING comes easy to them. ☹

Sometimes I wonder why Sophie even wants to be friends with me. Come to think of it, why would ANY of those smart kids want to be friends with me?

There's only ONE THING that I'm good at:

FASHION, FASHION, FASHION !!!!!!!!

I can design outfits in my sleep 24/7. ☺

But it's not like fashion design is going to help me pass Mrs. Marlow's math class. NOT. And it's certainly not going to help me get an A on Mr. Finkleman's solar energy quiz on Friday. NO WAY. ☹ ☹ ☹

That just reminds me, I have an AWESOME idea for a black skirt with stars on the pockets. It would look SO CHIC with a white blouse. If only I could find a way to make the stars glow in the dark—it might even get me a few bonus points if I wore it to science class. ☺ I need all the help I can get.

It's almost time to go to Sophie's house. She's helping me with my math this afternoon, and I'm quizzing her on random science questions for the big match. I may not know any of the answers, but I can at least help her practice! ☺

MORE LATER!!!

GO CRUSADERS!

Prayer List

1. Pray that my BFF won't be so stressed about stuff.
2. Pray that I can pass math and science. PLEEEZE!!!!
3. Be thankful to have a BFF who can tutor me!

WEDNESDAY, JANUARY 22

After practicing with Sophie yesterday, there's one thing I'm sure about: She is a GENIUS.

My best friend can hold more science stuff in her head than Einstein. When I asked her to name all the planets in the solar system, she listed ALL of them before I even finished asking the question! Or when I asked her to explain photosynthesis, she did it so well that EVEN I UNDERSTOOD IT!

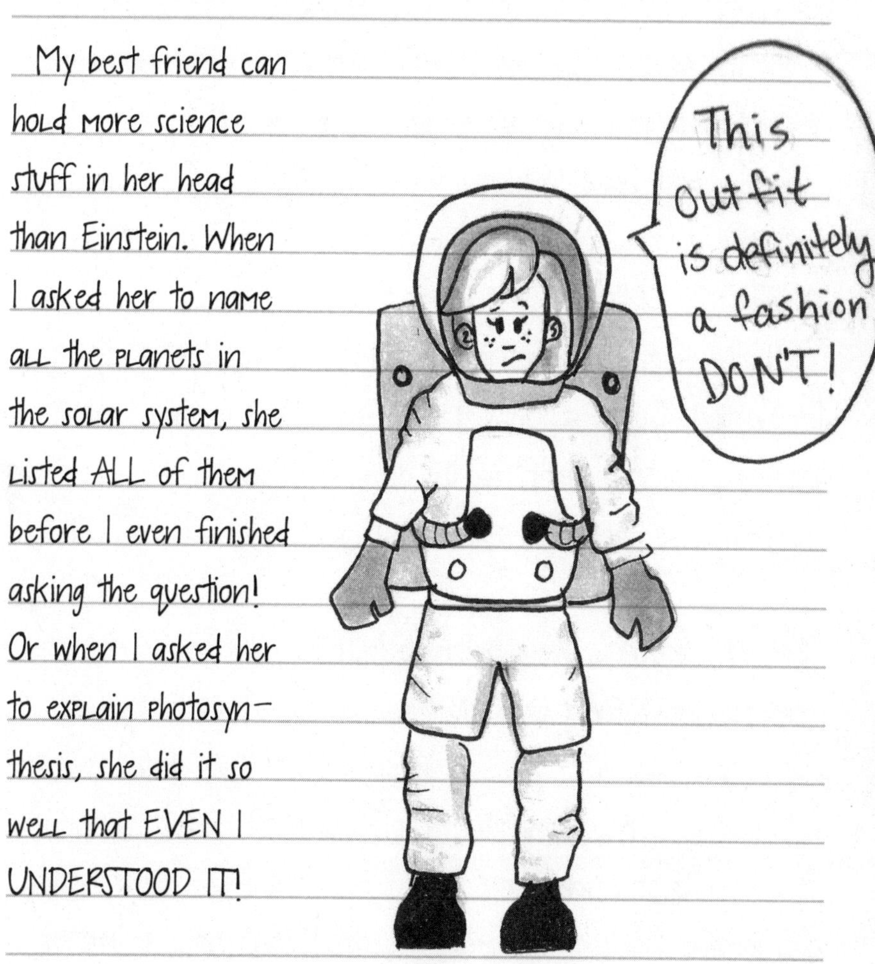

Sometimes I think Sophie could do a better job teaching me science than Mr. Finkleman. Or maybe it's just that Mr. Finkleman is **SUPER BORING.** I know he really tries, but I just don't get why we have to know all that stuff.

Why do I need to know about the phases of the moon if I'm not going to be an astronaut?

Or why do I have to know about the different "states of matter"? It really shouldn't matter! (get it? . . . MATTER?) LOL!!!!

Both Mom and Dad remind me that I still need to try and do my best. But what they don't understand is that I AM trying my best, er, most of the time, at least.

GRRRR . . . Sometimes my parents just DO NOT GET IT.

I'm not like all those brainiac kids.

And maybe I don't want to be.

After all, a few of the kids in class make fun of the brainiacs because they're so smart. Those rude kids make noises or roll their eyes whenever Sophie, Lauren, or Ian answer the questions during a quiz game. At least I don't have to put up with THAT. Being an art kid does have its positives. ☺

But who am I kidding? Miranda is one of the kids who make fun of Sophie and the others in the first place. **AND I'M ALREADY A PROFESSIONAL IN DEALING WITH MIRANDA MARONI.**

If I were a brainiac AND a fashion diva, she'd probably bully me into LEAVING TOWN. Thank goodness I'm just an art kid.

If I can pass math and science without being grounded, I consider that a WIN/WIN. Why can't every class be like Mrs. Gibson's art class? It's super easy to me, but Sophie totally dreads it.

And I love social studies, even though Sophie thinks it's totally boring. I don't think Emily or Miranda like it either, since both of them were nodding off in class today. Miranda was even drooling on her notebook.

GROOOOSSSS . . .

I can only imagine if that had been me. I'm sure Miranda would have snapped a pic with her phone and messaged everyone in her address book.

I thought social studies was really interesting today. Mrs. Bristow taught a cool lesson about India. She showed us pictures of incredible white marble buildings that don't look anything like the ones in America. Some even have elephants roaming around like it's the most normal thing ever.

STRANGE.

The Germ would go BONKERS if he lived there. Maybe I could talk him and Rosey into moving? LOL! ☺ I'm sure he already knows about Indian elephants anyway since he's such an animal freak.

Oh, and the fashions in India are A-M-A-Z-I-N-G! If only I owned a sari dress like the girls wear in New Delhi. I read all about them online. Saris are made of silk fabric and found at bazaars or markets all over the country. Why doesn't the mall in Clairemont sell this kind of stuff?

Maybe I'll design my own sari??

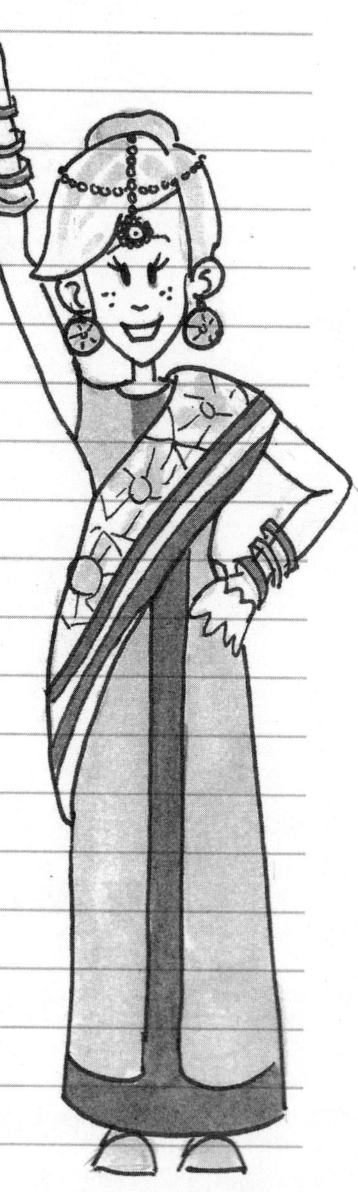

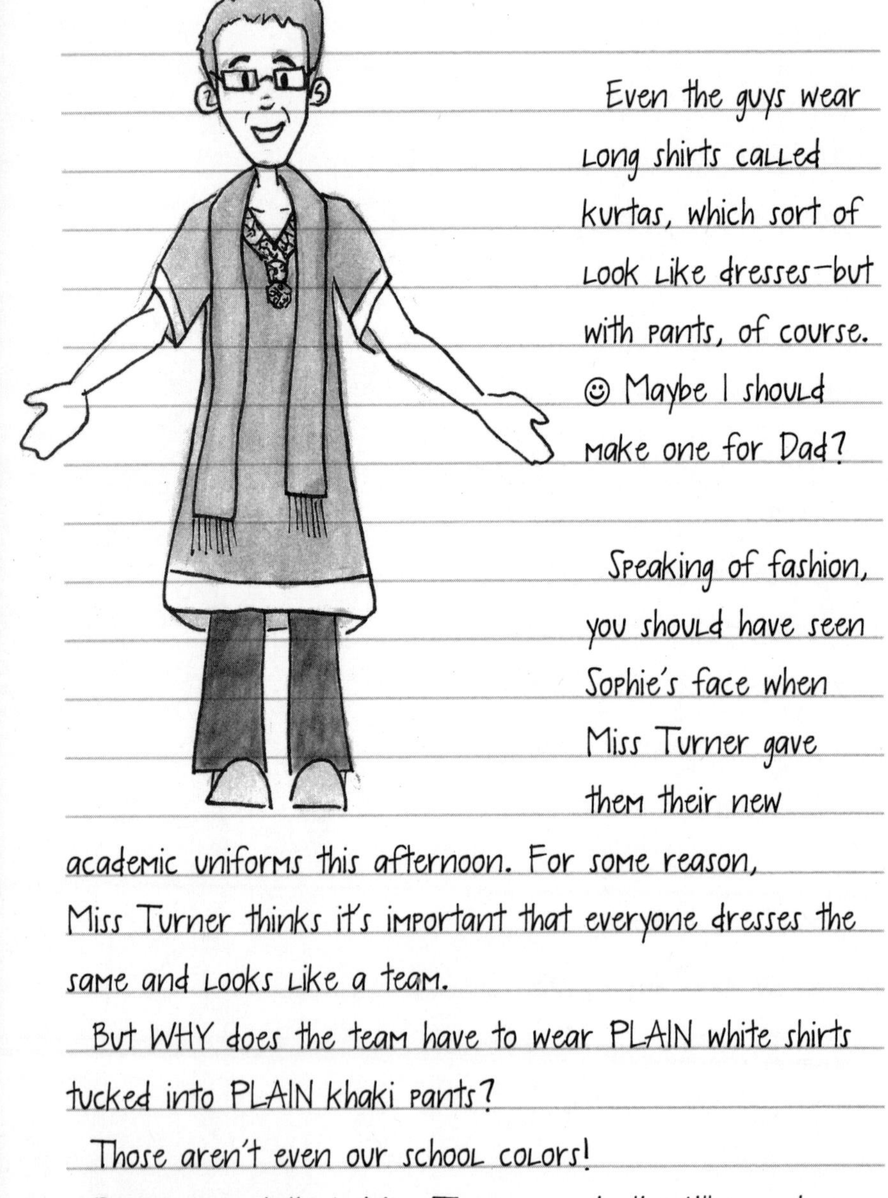

Even the guys wear long shirts called kurtas, which sort of look like dresses—but with pants, of course. ☺ Maybe I should make one for Dad?

Speaking of fashion, you should have seen Sophie's face when Miss Turner gave them their new academic uniforms this afternoon. For some reason, Miss Turner thinks it's important that everyone dresses the same and looks like a team.

But WHY does the team have to wear PLAIN white shirts tucked into PLAIN khaki pants?

Those aren't even our school colors!

Personally, I think Miss Turner needs the 411 on school fashion!

It's a good thing that Miranda Maroni was nowhere in sight when Sophie held up her uniform. That would have been THE WORST!

I could only imagine what RUDE things Miranda would say.

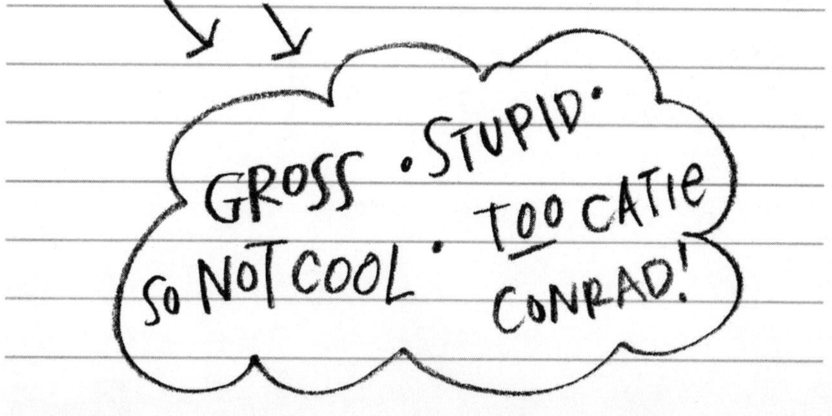

As soon as I got home, Sophie messaged me on the computer.

Sophie: Oh. My. Gosh. These uniforms r hideous!

Me: Sorry Soph, but I gotta agree with U. Miss Turner has definitely gone over the edge. That outfit looks like a golf uniform gone bad.

Sophie: I know, right? Ugh. But I really like being on the academic team, so I guess I'll just roll with it. C YA. Signed, EPIC FASHION FAILURE! Lol

But as soon as Sophie signed off, I suddenly got a BRILLIANT idea!

Hmmmm . . . maybe . . . just maybe . . . the Clairemont Crusaders could get a little makeover—courtesy of Catie Conrad! ☺

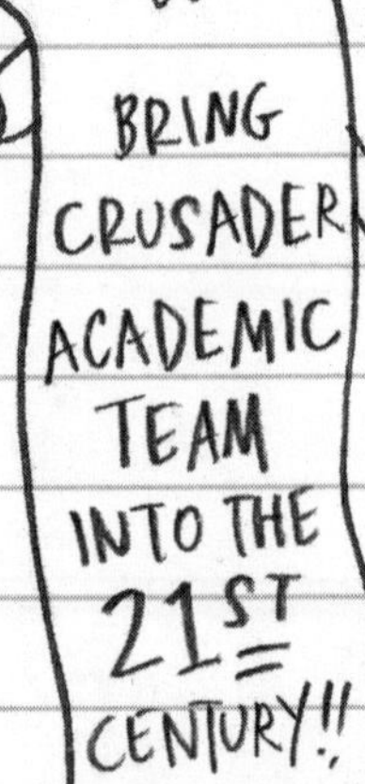

THURSDAY, JANUARY 23

I should have expected it. The GERM had to mess up a perfectly good afternoon. ☹

Really, it was sort of Mom's fault too. My irritating brother asked if he could invite his friend, Dylan Campbell, over today, and Mom said YES. ☹

I. COULD. NOT. BELIEVE. IT.

When I was eight, Mom NEVER let me have a play date over in the middle of the week! She always had an excuse: she was WAY too tired from work, we were WAY too busy, or I had WAY too much homework.

But the Germ can look up at Mom, bat those crazy long eyelashes, and Mom turns to mush.

UGH.

The baby of the family always gets it easier.

SO. NOT. FAIR.

Now the Germ has officially gone bonkers and is bouncing all over the house. You'd think that the president of *Animal Planet* was coming over or something. My goofy brother is even CLEANING HIS ROOM!

What's the big deal about Dylan coming over anyway?

And just when I was about to go to the pantry and grab a snack, the Germ practically knocked me over to get there first. ☹

"I HAVE to prepare a welcome feast for Dylan!" he said. Then he went on to get out gummy bears, gummy sharks, gummy worms, and oh, yeah, mac and cheese. Sometimes the Germ even puts the gummy bears IN his mac and cheese.

Yeah, I know. **WEIRD, WEIRD, WEIRD.**

The only safe thing to do now is to go to my room and hide!!!!

Maybe I'll just forget about it and design something . . . ANYTHING!

I still think the uniforms Sophie and her teammates are being forced to wear are totally sad looking. ☹ Who on earth designs stuff like that? That person must have been born in the '80s or something. If I thought Miss Turner would really listen to me, I'd try to design something the team would like better . . . WAY BETTER!!!

OR NOT . . .

I'm sure Miss Turner would think it was just a WEIRD IDEA from a WEIRD sixth grader who WASN'T even SMART enough to be on the academic team.

She'd probably listen if I'd taken Sophie's advice and asked to be on the team at the beginning of the year. THEN I'd be on her good side. But I chickened out.

MISS TURNER WOULDN'T HAVE WANTED A FASHION DIVA ON THE TEAM ANYWAY.

And who knows, maybe the rest of the team actually LIKES those uniforms? What if Lauren's favorite color is white? (Which makes no sense to me, since I LOVE COLOR! ☺)

Or maybe Zoey thinks khakis are cool?

So instead of worrying about giving some fashion flair to a Clairemont uniform, I think I'll forget about it and design something else:

GOOD-LUCK POSTERS!

If Miranda's precious volleyball team can put up "CRUSADERS RULE" posters, then why shouldn't the academic team have posters too?

RIGHT? ☺

MORE LATER!

I just heard the Germ and his little friend squealing at the top of their lungs. Surely there are earplugs around here somewhere. . . .

I CANNOT BELIEVE THIS!!!

I am SOOOOOOO glad that I have this diary to vent in, or else I'd EXPLODE!

I don't even know if I can write about it, but I'll try . . .

THE GERM and his friend, Dylan Campbell, are about to **PUSH ME OVER THE EDGE!**

Okay, so get this: Mom just informed me that Dylan and his family are adopting a baby from an orphanage in China. Yeah, it's awesome that they're getting Dylan a baby sister and everything. **BUT THAT'S NOT THE BAD PART.**

Their family is traveling to Beijing to pick her up and will be out of town for over two weeks. . . . **THAT'S NOT THE BAD PART EITHER.**

AND since Dylan can't take his pet with him, they've asked the Germ to pet sit. AND, by pet sit, I'm not talking about feeding a goldfish or a hamster like most NORMAL people. Dylan has to be the kid with a

BEARDED DRAGON LIZARD!!!

And get this—its name is Binky! **BINKY!!!** A creepy lizard that looks like something from Jurassic Park has the same name of my baby pacifier!

GROSS, GROSS, DOUBLE GROSS!

THAT'S why the Germ was so excited about Dylan Campbell coming over. DUH. I should have known it would have something to do with weird animals. And no wonder the Germ was cleaning up his room. He was PREPARING FOR THE NEXT CREATURE!

OH. MY. GOODNESS.

You should have heard the Germ introducing Rosey to Binky.

"Binky, this is Rosey, and she is soooo sweet. Now, don't harm her and she won't harm you. I've made a place for your aquarium right beside my bed so I can keep an eye on you. I've even got your cricket snacks and salad ready. You're going to love it here."

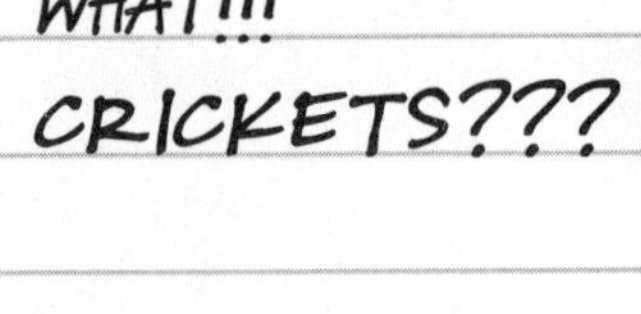

UGH.

You have GOT to be KIDDING ME!

Then the Germ REALLY did it. I actually heard him say with my very own ears: "And Binky, I promise that my grouchy sister won't bother you. She really needs a cage worse than you do. She is SUCH a pest."

EWWW!

The Germ is calling ME a pest? **ME?????**

Oh, I cannot WAIT until Dad gets home. Hopefully Sophie is home too—I MUST vent to someone about this!

How on earth am I gonna finish these academic posters with a bug-eating lizard on the loose?

GERM + SKUNK + BEARDED DRAGON LIZARD =

TOTAL INSANITY!

EMERGENCY

Prayer List

1. Pray that I'm not attacked and eaten by a DISGUSTING reptile!
2. Pray that I don't act so jealous over my PEST of a brother.
3. Pray that I don't go INSANE over the next few weeks because our house has turned into a **ZOO**!

FRIDAY, JANUARY 24

Sophie didn't even respond to my DESPERATE message last night! ☹

I could have used someone to stick up for me since Dad certainly DIDN'T.

Anti-Bearded-Dragon Me: Dad, the last thing we need around this house is another animal! And you never know WHEN that crazy skunk is gonna pounce. For all I know she might even try to EAT Binky!

Lizard-Loving Dad: Catie, you're just going to have to calm down. Jeremy will keep a good eye on them both. He does have a special touch with animals, you know. I'll make sure he doesn't let Binky bother you.

Still-Frustrated Me: The Germ bothers me EVERY SINGLE DAY OF MY LIFE! He's a bigger pest than what that ugly lizard's going to be! Why couldn't Dylan have picked some OTHER kid to pet sit that ridiculous reptile? WHY?

Still-Lizard-Loving Dad: Catherine, that's not a very nice thing to say about your brother—or Binky for that matter. You're blessed to have a little brother and need to remember that. Dylan and his family are traveling all the way to China to get a new member for their family. Don't you think God wants us to be a little more understanding?

UGH. I knew to give up after that.

Dad was right.

But I didn't sleep a wink from worrying about that lizard lurking around the house and crawling underneath my door.

I think I may have to drink some of Mom's coffee to help wake me up before school!

Thanks for nothing Binky—you're ALREADY driving me CRAZY after just one night!

More later . . . **IF I SURVIVE!!!!!**

Z Z Z Z Z Z Z Z Z . . .

SOOOO SLEEPY . . .

I barely made it through the entire day at school. Sophie had to nudge me with a pencil in three different classes just to keep my eyes open.

It was ALL the Germ's fault.

Sleep deprivation is probably why I also flunked Mr. Finkleman's science quiz today. ☹ We'd been studying the periodic table, and it was SUPER BORING, not to mention SUPER CONFUSING.

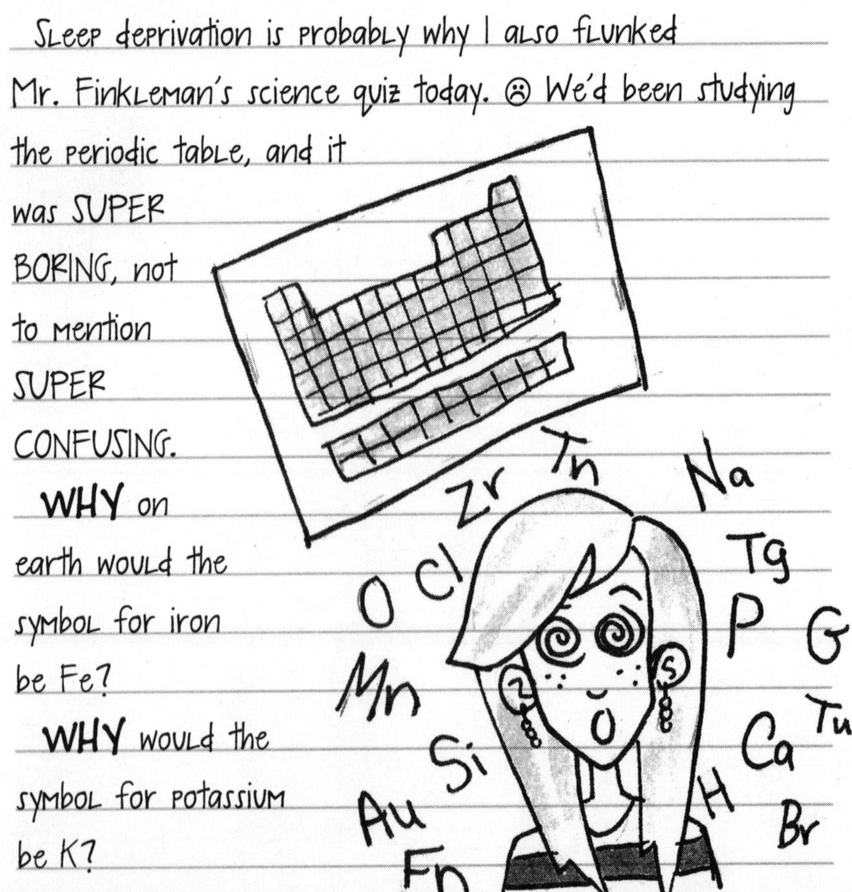

WHY on earth would the symbol for iron be Fe?

WHY would the symbol for potassium be K?

AND **WHY** did Mr. Finkleman count off on my paper when I wrote "So" for sodium? He said it was Na!

WHY? WHY? WHY!!!!!!!

There's not even an N or an A in the word SODIUM!

I guess it's just ONE MORE THING that Sophie gets to help me with after school. She'll probably get sick of helping me one of these days. ☹

But Sophie did like the posters I put up at break. Actually, everyone on the team thought they were cool. Even Mrs. Gibson, the most awesome art teacher in the history of awesome art teachers, stopped in the hall and said they were "expressive and uplifting"!

I think that meant she liked them. ☺

Of course there was ONE person who made sure that I overheard HER opinion on things: ***MIRANDA MARONI.***

Naturally.

"Hey, Catie, did you really draw those posters in the hall?" Miranda asked, smiling.

WEIRD.

She actually sounded sort of . . . NICE.

Maybe Miranda had become a fan of my work? Maybe I'll design a gym bag for that volleyball of hers? She bounces it through the hall enough. But as soon as I was about to say, "Why, yes, thank you, Miranda. Yes, I did draw those posters," MIRANDA INTERRUPTED ME.

"Oh, yeah, I can see it now, Conrad. You DEFINITELY did those posters. The letters are lopsided, and the colors are all wrong. Of course you did those," she said, staring straight at me.

UGH. ☹

SHE DRIVES ME INSANE.

Luckily, Sophie jerked me by the arm and pulled me on to art class. "Just pray for her, Catie," she whispered. "You know how she is."

BUT it is soooooo HARD!!!

I kept repeating Galations 6:9 in my head.

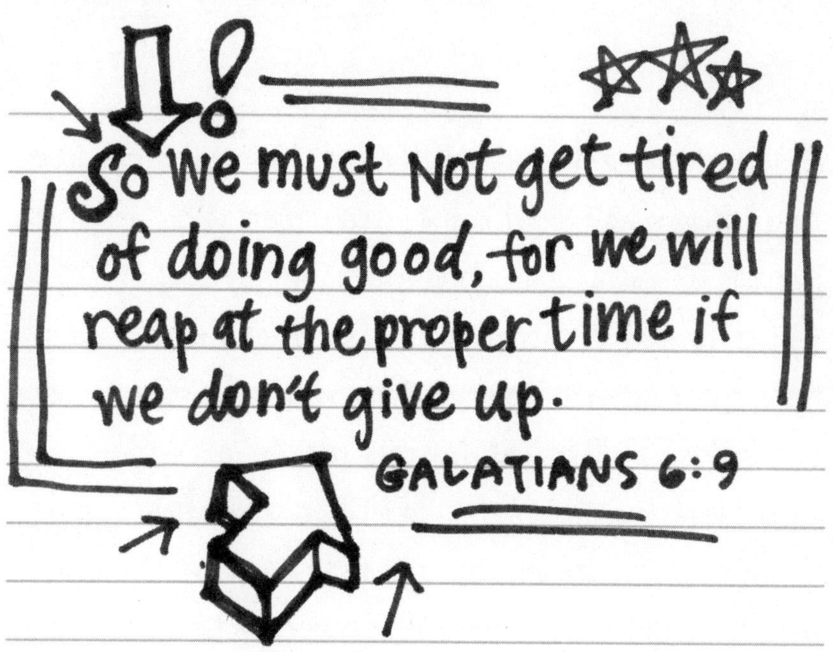

At least I was going to art class. ☺ I can forget almost every problem I have by just walking into Mrs. Gibson's room. Even if Miranda Maroni, aka "the art critic," didn't have anything nice to say about my art, I knew Mrs. Gibson liked it.

Today we studied landscape art and looked at a bunch of haystacks by Monet. Every single one looked just a little different, depending on the time of day he painted it. Mrs. Gibson also showed paintings by Vincent van Gogh, her favorite artist of all time. ***Starry Night*** was definitely my favorite. But I also like the one of the church, even though it did look kinda dark. Maybe he was depressed about something? Maybe he'd met Miranda's long-lost ancestor? Then I could TOTALLY understand why he was so sad!

After looking at the paintings, Mrs. Gibson handed out pastels and asked us to draw our own version of a landscape. SWEET! That sounded easy enough, and I could hardly wait to get started. I decided on a mountain scene and used blues, greens, and browns. For added effect, I even put bright yellow swirls in the sky, sort of like van Gogh did in some of his paintings.

But Josh and Sophie didn't even know where to start. Sophie sat there with the blankest look on her face ever.

Josh stared at me like I was a total weirdo. He'd probably heard I flunked that quiz on the periodic table, which should have been easy-easy for anyone but ME. Still, he just sat there with this strange look on his face.

What was with him???

I tried to weasel it out of Sophie after class.

Confused Me: Soph, what was up with you-know-who in art class?

Soph: What do you mean?

STILL-Confused Me: You know! J.H. wouldn't even speak to me. He just sat there and stared. I don't get it!

Soph: Oh, THAT! Get this: Josh said you were the BEST artist he'd ever seen, and he was embarrassed to draw around you because you were so GOOD.

FREAKED-OUT ME: NO. WAY. Are you SERIOUS?

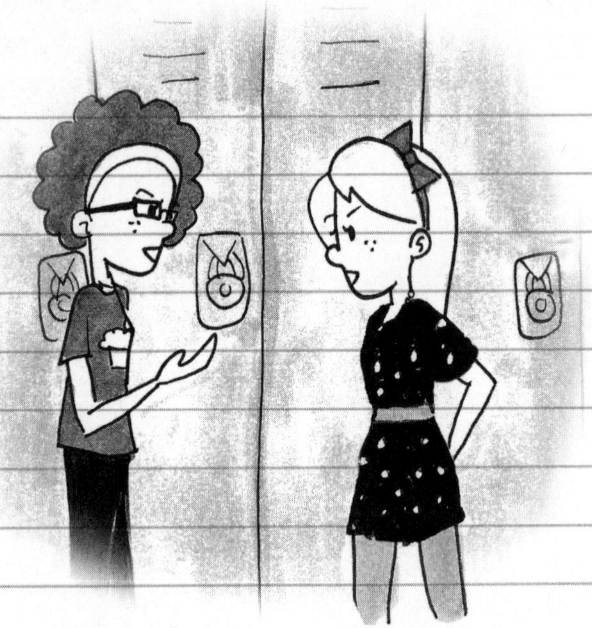

Soph: Uh huh, I'm serious. Why would I lie to you? You're my BEST FRIEND, remember? And since you're my BFF, you had better be at that academic match tomorrow! I need all the support I can get!

ADD TO PRAYER LIST:

1. Sophie and the entire academic team.
2. BINKY—pray he will stay away from me ENTIRELY.

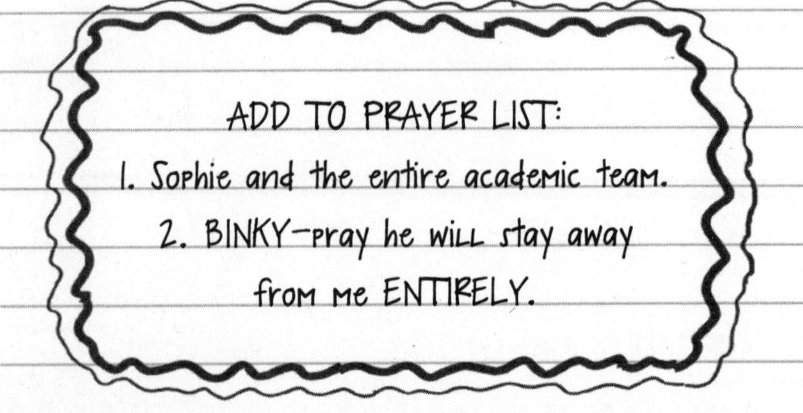

SATURDAY, JANUARY 25

I could hardly wait to get to the big match today. Mom even dropped me off early so I could wish Sophie good luck.

I also thought it was VERY IMPORTANT to dress in our school colors: blue, white, and silver. I quickly sewed together a GORGEOUS blue-and-white striped scarf that looked great with my black sweater. I even slid on three silver bracelets and a pair of silver earrings to complete my look. A girl MUST accessorize after all! ☺

After wishing my BFF good luck, I looked over and noticed that **J.H.** and our friend Tyler were in the bleachers! *What were they doing there?* **STRANGE.** Since it was Saturday, I figured they were home glued to their video games. Or had ball practice.

I sat down in the only open seat beside Tyler. WHEW! We'd become good friends ever since he moved to our school last year. I felt WAY better sitting beside him and NOT JOSH. If I had to sit near my secret crush, I'm sure that:

A. My mouth would go dry.
B. The water fountain wouldn't work, and I'd pass out in front of everyone.
C. My brain would go totally blank, and I'd forget his name.

Yeah, none of the three options were good.

Luckily the match got started on time, and I could concentrate on something else **BESIDES J.H.** We all applauded when Sophie, Lauren, Ian, and Zoey walked onto the stage and took their seats.

Then out walked Whitman Middle School's team. None of them cracked a smile. THEY. MEANT. BUSINESS.

After both sides tested the buzzer system, the moderator began asking questions. You could have heard a pin drop in that auditorium.

It didn't take but a few questions to identify the kid Sophie had described. I've never seen a guy do math problems so quickly! I mean, REALLY, he solved a percentage problem before the moderator even finished the question! And I almost fell out of my seat when he did an "area of a parallelogram" problem in about five seconds.

I can't even SPELL the word P.A.R.A.L.L.E.L.O.G.R.A.M.

I felt so sorry for Sophie. I knew that she knew a lot of those answers. It was just that the kid from Whitman knew them a little faster. ☹

BUT Sophie let 'em have it when it came to the science stuff!

THAT'S MY BFF!!!!!

She knew every bone of the skeletal system and beat Whitman at the buzzer on every question about the periodic table. (I'm glad SOMEONE understood it!)

And when they got to the questions about earthquakes and volcanoes, you'd have thought Sophie was some kind of geologist or something.

MY BFF ROCKED!!!

The rest of the team was awesome too. Lauren buzzed in before anyone when the moderator asked those "name the musical composer" questions, and Ian knew EVERYTHING about *Artemis Fowl* and *The Book Thief*.

There were only a few minutes left in the match, and my heart was racing!

That's when Zoey answered two of the most RANDOM THINGS EVER: one minute she knew the name of the river that runs through Paris, and the next she was answering questions about ancient Chinese dynasties.

And guess what?

WE WON!!!!!!!!!!!!!!!!

I suddenly wished I were on the academic team. ☹

"One down and one to go!" Sophie said after the match. "Then it's the district championship! You guys better be there. I think you're bringing me good luck—I wasn't even nervous today!"

That made one of us. . . .

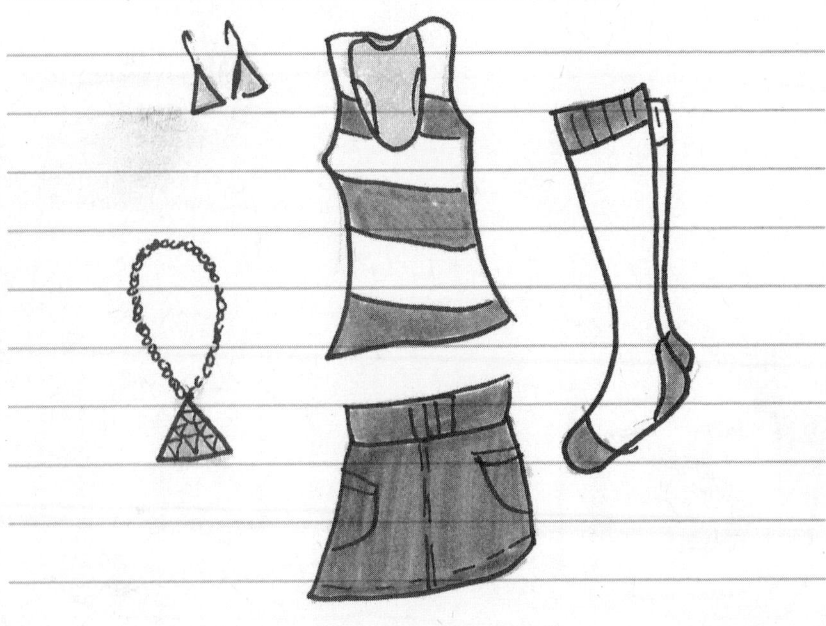

SUNDAY, JANUARY 26

UGH.

Even our Sunday school teacher remembered that Valentine's Day is coming up. ☹

Mrs. Childers had written our names on pink and red paper hearts and taped them all over the door. It was sort of cool I guess—ESPECIALLY when I noticed that Josh's red heart was within inches of my pink one. ☺

He probably didn't even notice. . . .

Sometimes Josh is even one of my unspoken prayer requests. What else can I do but pray about it?

Today Mrs. Childers made a prayer list on the board and asked if any of us had a request to say out loud. Sophie was the first to raise her hand, "My dad has gotten really stressed out at work. Can we add him to the list?"

It was a no-brainer that Mr. Martin would be stressed. Being a principal had to be the worst job ever. Who would want to deal with a bunch of yelling kids all day?

I raised my hand next. *"For Dylan's family to have a safe trip to China. Oh, and can I add one more, Mrs. Childers? To have lots more patience with my brother and this whole pet-sitting thing."*

Many people at church knew that Dylan's family was adopting a baby in China. But hardly anyone knew there was another member of Dylan's family—a BEARDED DRAGON—that was now part of MY FAMILY for a while—**whether I liked it or not!** ☹

GRRR . . .

I need all the prayers I can get.

"You know, Catie," said Mrs. Childers, "we talked about biblical examples of patience just a few weeks ago. Remember how frustrated Sarah was? She had to be patient about something more important than a new pet. She and Abraham waited a long time for a child. And didn't God work everything out for good?"

My teacher had a point. And I couldn't help but think about the real reason the Germ was pet-sitting Binky in the first place—so the Campbells could adopt a baby from China. I'm sure they wanted a baby as much as Sarah wanted a child. I wonder if Mrs. Childers knew that already?

Since Dylan's family goes to our church, Dad received an update from our pastor on how things were going.

"It sounds like they made it to Beijing just fine," Dad said on the way home. "It takes quite a while to fill out all the paperwork and get the documentation ready. But it's such a blessing they're bringing this baby into a loving Christian home."

Sure, but my first question was: "WHEN IS DYLAN COMING BACK TO PICK UP THAT GROSS-LOOKING LIZARD?"

And when we got home from church, my prayer for patience was put to the test in TWO SECONDS.

That didn't take long. ☹

In his typical annoying way, the Germ barged into my room, grabbed my bottle of Sweet Sugar body spray, and marched out as quickly as he came in.

WEIRD. WEIRD. DOUBLE WEIRD.

Since when did my brother want to smell like dessert?

Annoyed Me: What do you think you're DOING?! I know you stink, but do you REALLY want to smell like a girl?

Weird Germ: NOT funny. YOU'RE the one who stinks! And for your information, I poured out that smelly stuff and filled the bottle with water. Binky needs his skin misted and kept moist as much as possible. You know, it's a lizard kind of thing.

FURIOUS Me: You did WHAT? I am SO telling Mom! You're going to be in BIG trouble because of that FREAK of a reptile!

Know-It-All Germ: Actually, his scientific name is Pogona vitticeps. And if you keep showing anger like that, he's going to flare out his neck as a defense mechanism. That'll show you!

Even-MORE-Furious Me: WHO CARES! You better get your OWN defense mechanism if that lizard goes into my room!

Ridiculous Germ: The guy on the Leapin' Lizards TV show says bearded dragons can live up to twenty years. I think I'll ask Mom for one after Dylan picks up Binky.

This is not happening. . . . I repeat. . . . this CANNOT be happening. . . .

GRRRR . . .

HOW CAN GOD BE SO PATIENT WITH A KID AS IRRITATING AS MY BROTHER??!!!!!

Surely Mom will take up for me this time after I inform her that her son is actually a **THIEF!**

But I don't know if Mom and Dad heard a single word I said. Both of them were practically glued to the computer screen.

STRANGE.

I'd never seen them both look so serious about something. ODD. . . .

"I think we should encourage Jeremy to give up part of his allowance for this, don't you?" Dad said.

They must have heard me after all! YES!!!!

"I agree, dear," Mom chimed in. "After all, it's the right thing to do. We'll talk with him and Catie about it at dinner."

FINALLY! I knew they'd see the REAL Jeremy one of these days!

I can hardly wait to see the Germ's face when he finds out that part of his allowance money has to buy girly stuff! ☺☺☺

THIS IS GOING TO BE PRICELESS! I might even bring my camera to the dinner table so I can capture the moment!

More later! I suddenly feel like drawing!

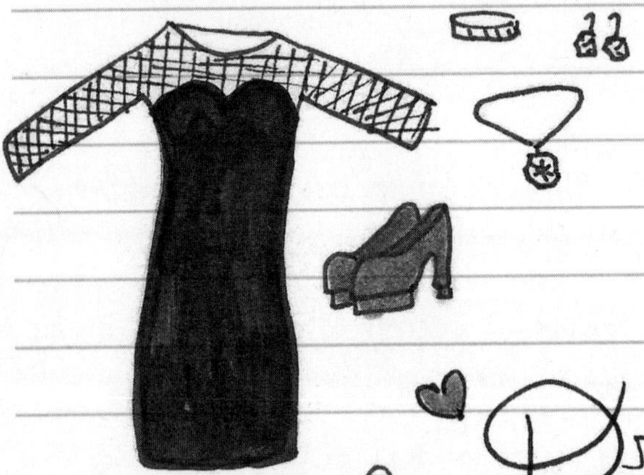

Dreamy

LBD!

(Little Black Dress)

Dinner was NOT AT ALL what I expected.

Not only did my parents NOT punish the Germ for throwing away my favorite body spray, but they also allowed him to bring Binky to the dinner table.

☹☹☹☹

WHAT WAS WITH MY PARENTS????

Instead of grounding the Germ, Dad told us all about the new article he's working on for the magazine. Dylan's family gave him lots of info on international adoptions, and after doing a little research online, he and Mom decided we should sponsor a needy child in another country.

So THAT'S why they'd been glued to the computer.

Dad asked the Germ and me to even consider pitching in some of our allowance to help.

HUH??

"Would you like a few days to pray about this?" Mom asked. "You know, to search your heart and talk to God about it. That's perfectly fine."

Hmmmm . . .

I always use my allowance to buy fashion stuff—sketch pencils, fabric, buttons, etc. After all, if I'm going to be the next FASHION DESIGNER TO THE STARS, I need to have materials.

But Mom was right. Maybe I really needed to pray about this sponsorship stuff.

"Your mom and I have been reading about an organization called Compassion International," Dad said. "We can even look at photos, pick out a country, and choose a specific child."

That sounded interesting . . . but also confusing. "How can we pick out just one kid when obviously tons of kids need stuff?" I asked.

"It would be wonderful if we could help out every orphanage and every child, but that's impossible financially," said Dad. "Jesus said, 'Whatever you do for the least of these, you do for me.' So your Mom and I think we should all do our part."

I needed to check out the website that Dad was talking about. It was hard for me to believe that we could actually SEE the kid who we'd be sponsoring on the other side of the planet.

That might be really cool.

"Mom, may I hurry and finish dinner and get on the computer?" I asked. "I'm not really hungry and want to check out that website."

Anyway, it was all I could do to swallow Mom's lasagna while looking at the Germ and that reptile perched on his shoulder. Thankfully he'd at least kept Rosey in his room.

He knew we'd all go crazy if he brought BOTH of those WEIRD CREATURES to the table.

I could NOT believe that so many kids live in orphanages or really poor homes until I saw it for myself.

Whoa. ☹ ☹

Some of the kids had parents but needed money to grow gardens for food. Some of them had no family due to sickness or wars, and they needed medicine and clothes.

STRANGE. I never really thought about needing a garden so I could eat. Mom just always drives to the market and buys stuff. I'd also never thought about needing money to get my medicine. Dad just usually picks it up at the pharmacy.

After reading about all of this on Dad's computer, I didn't need to pray about my allowance.

Just by looking at all those kids, I could tell that they needed anything we could send. I told Mom and Dad that I was all in on the project.

Maybe I'll tell Sophie about it too. Maybe she's never even heard of Compassion International. Hopefully she'll be at her computer and get my message.

Excited Me: Hey, Soph. You won't believe what happened tonight. The Germ and I are gonna get a brother or sister! Well . . . sort of, that is.

Shocked Sophie: WHAT? How do you "sort of" get a brother or sister? YOU. R. STRANGE. LOL!

Excited Me Again: LOL. What I mean is we're going to sponsor a kid and send him money to buy things he needs. You know, like food, medicine, and stuff. We're even going to look at pictures and pick out a child from this website. I know it sounds weird, but

Mom says it's a good way to help. I'll get the 411 and tell you about it 2morrow.

Brilliant Soph: OHHHHH, I get it. Sounds cool! BTW, don't forget about that quiz on Asia tomorrow. Ugh. BOR-ING. ☹

Relieved Me: OMG. I total forgot! Thanx Soph! But I think I remember most of that stuff. I was online the other night reading about it.

Shocked Sophie: Okay, now you're REALLY strange. U LIKE reading about Asia? Am I messaging the correct Catie Conrad?

Fashionable Me: LOL. You should read about the fashions in India and China—they R AMAZING!

BFF Sophie: I should have KNOWN this had something to do with you and your FASHIONS! C U 2morrow. NOW GO STUDY!

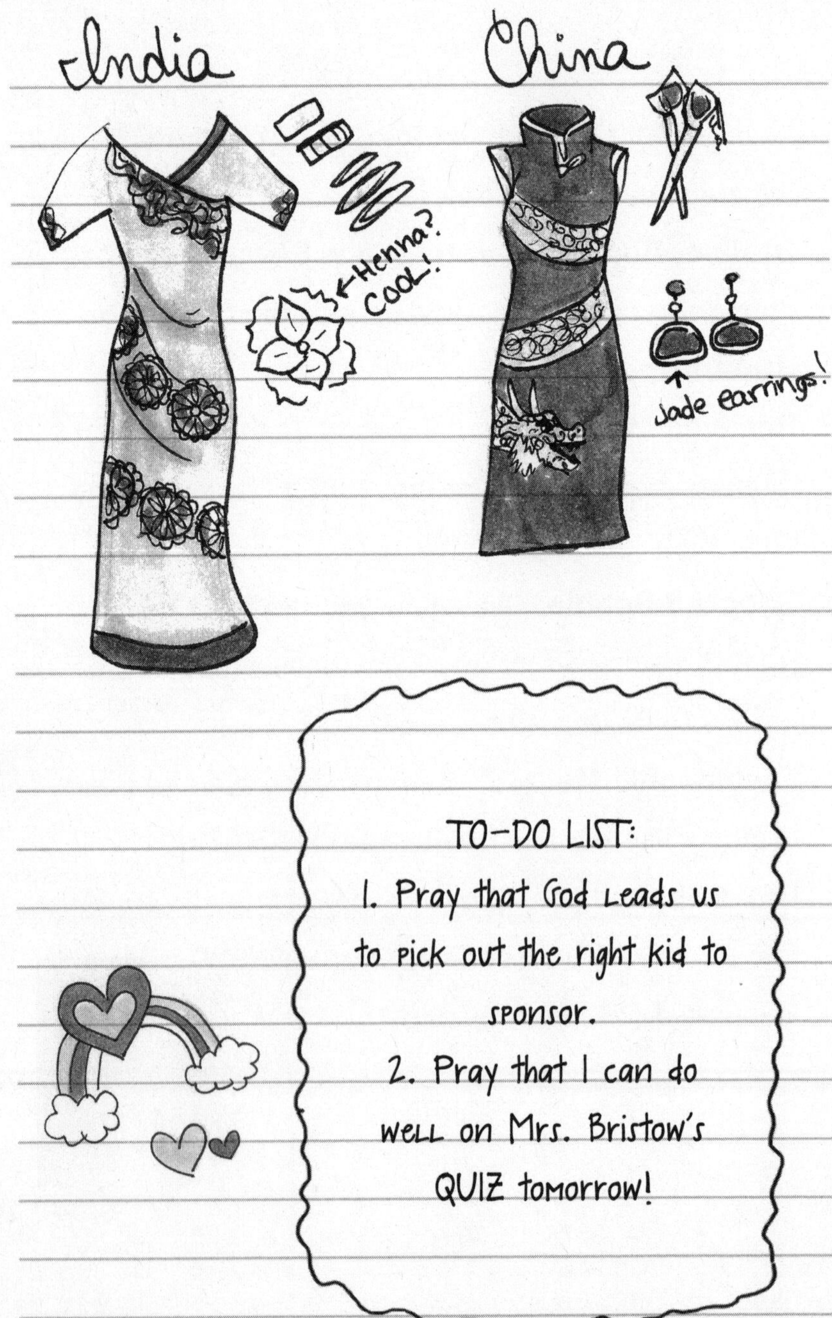

TO-DO LIST:

1. Pray that God leads us to pick out the right kid to sponsor.
2. Pray that I can do well on Mrs. Bristow's QUIZ tomorrow!

MONDAY, JANUARY 27

TODAY MY LIFE WAS:

AWESOME!!!!!!!!!!!!! ☺

AND

HORRIBLE. ☹☹☹

ALL at the same time!!!

Of course, ANYTHING that has to do with AWESOMENESS usually means one of the following:

1. I ACE a test at school. (But not in math or science—the possibility of acing a test in those classes is ZERO.)
2. I come up with the PERFECT fashion design.
3. The Germ, Binky, and Rosey leave me alone . . . or better yet LEAVE THE STATE!
4. *Miranda Maroni* switches schools.
5. JOSH HENDERSON talks to me.

The first thing I had to do this morning was take Mrs. Bristow's quiz on Asia. Sophie totally freaked out about it, probably because it had nothing to do with math or science.

Secretly, it felt sort of good that I was better than Sophie at something. Social studies is one of the few classes where I actually feel a little smart.

Since I'd been designing international fashions in my sketchbook, I'd also been reading about India and China online. And hey, who knows, maybe the kid we're going to sponsor from Compassion International will be from one of those countries!

Whether it was fill-in-the-blank or matching, I knew the answer to every single question on that quiz.

In fact:

When Mrs. Bristow handed back our papers at the end of class, she'd written "Excellent, Catie! I think you're going to be a world traveler! ☺" at the top of the page.

Mrs. Bristow even announced to the whole class: "Congratulations, Catie Conrad, you made the top score on the quiz. Nice job!"

Sophie reached back and gave me a high five. ☺

Of course, Miranda made a weird snort like she didn't believe it. And naturally, Emily did the same thing. That girl is like Miranda's little puppet. UGH!

After class, Sophie showed me her paper at our lockers. I could tell she wasn't happy about it . . . at all. She'd received an 86/B on Mrs. Bristow's quiz.

It's-Not-a-Big-Deal Me: Why would ANYONE be upset over that? I would be SOOO HAPPY if I could get a B in Finkleman's science class!

Depressed BFF: I don't know what I'm going to do. When Mom finds out I got a B on this quiz, she is going to FREAK. I'll be grounded for at least a week.

Shocked Me: Over a B? You have GOT to be kidding! Your mom should see my grades in science! If you ask me, a B is really good! Anyway, you've been busy studying and WINNING for the academic team. She needs to give you a break.

Depressed BFF: That's just it. She said if I'm going to be captain of the academic team, I should make straight A's. It's really stressing me out.

BFF ME: You ARE trying, and that's what counts, right? That's what you tell me every time I flunk one of Finkleman's quizzes. Let's just pray that she chills out a little. That's all we can do.

My little pep talk seemed to help Sophie, so that was good. But then something happened that almost **PUT ME IN SHOCK!**

While Sophie and I were putting our social studies books back into our lockers, JOSH STOPPED BY AND SPOKE TO ME.

I TOTALLY FROZE.

"Hey, Catie," he said. "Any tips on acing that next social studies quiz? I stink at this kind of stuff. I'm more of a math person, I guess."

HUH? Josh Henderson wanted MY HELP on something?

"Uh . . . well . . . uh . . ." I said, sounding like a zombie. "Uh . . . maybe . . . uh . . ."

"MAYBE she can help you one day after school! RIGHT, CATIE?" Sophie said, coming in for the save.

"Oh, yeah, RIGHT!" I said. (I could sooo feel my face turning BRIGHT RED.)

"I think Mrs. Bristow does tutoring on Wednesdays," said Sophie. "I should probably go myself after that last quiz! Catie, maybe you can stay and help both of us. Right, Josh?"

"Yeah, that'd be cool," he said. "Thanks, Catie. Oh, and uh, you, too, Sophie. See ya."

And then Josh SMILED DIRECTLY AT ME and walked on down the hall.

THIS WAS THE BEST DAY OF MY LIFE!

I wouldn't have even known what to say if Sophie hadn't snapped me out of it. I'd probably still be standing there like a zombie. And the fact that Sophie VOLUNTEERED to stay after school too (since she knew I'd be SOOO NERVOUS) reminded me of what an INCREDIBLE BFF she really is.

When it comes to Josh Henderson, I don't know what happens to me. **I FREAK!** My mind goes blank, I get so dizzy, and I'm suddenly more clueless than ever.

And now I'm going to be helping my secret crush with his homework in just TWO DAYS!

My chances of focusing on anything else for the rest of the day were ZERO.

sequin flats-
too much?

Too
Casual?

ALL I could think about was:

WHAT ON EARTH AM I GOING TO WEAR ON WEDNESDAY?

Should I go with a dress? Or is that overdoing it?

Skinny jeans and a sweatshirt? Or is that too SLOPPY?

Accessories?

Should I wear my hair up?

DOWN?

Or down?

I'M DEFINITELY going to need Sophie's help on this!

I could hardly wait to go home and look through my closet. After all, a fashion designer must have appropriate tutoring-a-boy-for-a-quiz attire.

Right? ☺ ☺ ☺

BUT THEN THE HORRIBLE PART OF MY DAY HAPPENED. ☹

As soon as I got home from school, there was a message from Sophie on the computer.

Sophie: Okay, before I tell u this, u have to promise NOT to freak out.

Catie: Uh, okaaaay . . .

I won't freak out. SO TELL ME.

Sophie: Matt just texted me. When he was on his way to the gym for ball practice, he overheard Miranda telling some of her friends that you'd cheated on Mrs. Bristow's quiz.

Sophie: Remember, u promised not to freak. Who cares what Miranda thinks! Anyone who knows u knows u wouldn't cheat on a quiz. God knows the real u, and that's what's important. TTYL. I have to tell Mom that I got a B on that quiz. ☹ I'LL PRAY FOR YOU, AND YOU PRAY FOR ME! Later . . .

This had become **THE WORST DAY EVER!!!**

There's no way I can show my face in class tomorrow. By the time Miranda and Emily finish spreading their lies, my life will be **OVER**. ☹

All I wanted to do was go to my bedroom and try to calm down. I'll admit I cried a little too. HOW COULD SHE? I needed to pray about this, but I didn't even know what to say to God. Then I remembered what my Sunday school teacher had read to us from Matthew—that God knows what we need before we even ask Him. ***THANK GOODNESS!***

It felt good TRYING to turn everything over to God. BUT. IT. WAS. HARD.

If only my life weren't such a DISASTER.

And speaking of disasters, the Germ made my life an even BIGGER one this afternoon.

☹ As I was lying on my bed, trying to talk to God about stuff, I felt something crawling on my big toe. . . .

AND. THEN. IT. JUMPED!

A CRICKET!!!!

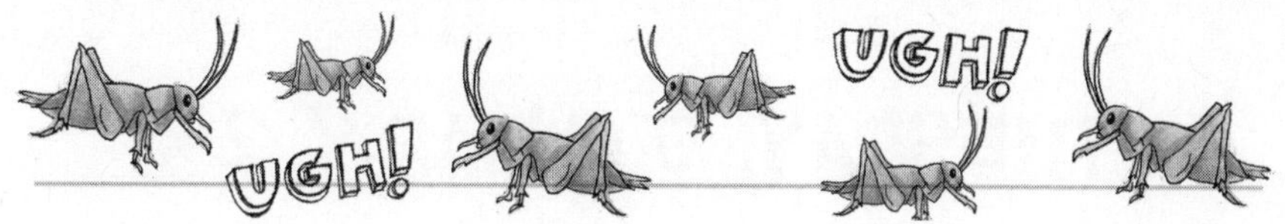

Did I mention that I DETEST bugs???

One of Binky's gross, hopping, crawly snack creatures was loose in my bedroom. And within TEN SECONDS I saw another one sitting on my sewing machine—and then on my sketchbook! **THEY WERE EVERYWHERE!**

~~ARGGGGHHHH~~!!!!!!! My room is DESTROYED!

I cannot WAIT until Mom gets home. Someway, somehow, I have GOT to calm down about this.

DEFINITELY ADD TO MY PRAYER LIST:

1. Thank God for having a best friend like Sophie Martin who always has my back—even when J.H. is involved. ☺
2. TRY AS HARD AS POSSIBLE to have patience with Miranda as well as my brother. (This is NOT going to be easy.)
3. Thank God that He understands my problems and is here to talk to about every single thing!

TUESDAY, JANUARY 28

I'm clueless on what I'm going to say to Miranda today. How can I look at her in the face, knowing she's spread a HUGE lie about me?

I even woke up an hour earlier than I had to this morning because I couldn't get it off my mind. It didn't help any that I was almost POSITIVE a few of those crickets were still hiding out in my room, even though Mom had made the Germ catch them all.

One pest was just as bad at the other. ☹

But writing in this diary sometimes helps me think a little more clearly. I also prayed that God would give me some guidance on how to handle girls who make up stuff just to be M-E-A-N.

I just don't get it.

I even broke down and talked to Mom about it last night—AFTER I'd told her about the Germ's crickets taking over my room!

Even though I wasn't sure if Mom knew what she was talking about, she said that Miranda might actually be JEALOUS of me!

BUT WHY???

Miranda has great hair. I have bad hair days at least three times a week.

Miranda has the latest and greatest of EVERYTHING. I usually have to wait until it's on sale and use my allowance.

Miranda wears makeup like those girls in the fashion magazines. I'm only allowed lip gloss and a little blush.

Miranda acts like NOTHING bothers her. Things bother me A LOT.

But Mom also reminded me of Matthew 5:39—

BUT I TELL YOU, DON'T RESIST AN EVILDOER. ON THE CONTRARY, IF ANYONE SLAPS YOU ON YOUR RIGHT CHEEK, TURN THE OTHER TO HIM ALSO.

SHEESH! 

Mom went on to explain that this verse meant I should just try to ignore her and not say anything back. TALK ABOUT HARD. I don't think she understands just how tough that's going to be with Miranda Maroni.

But I have to trust that God understands. He sees what's going on and will work this out . . . SOMEHOW.

More later. GOTTA GO FACE YOU-KNOW-WHO. ☹ ☹

I could feel my heart beating in my chest when I walked toward Mrs. Bristow's room this morning. I'd even put on extra deodorant, just in case I went into hyper sweat mode.

Luckily, Sophie was with me and kept repeating, "Remember, Catie, just ignore her." I also kept trying to remind myself of Matthew 5:39.

What if Miranda's lie had spread through the entire sixth grade? What if I walked in and everyone gave me "the look" like I was the most dishonest girl in the whole school?

WHAT IF JOSH HATED ME NOW?

By the time we got to class, Miranda was already there and, of course, acted TOTALLY INNOCENT like she hadn't done anything wrong.

GRRR . . .

She was even smiling and laughing with Emily about some-thing . . . probably something about ME. ☹

I also tried to get up the nerve to say hi to Josh. If he smiled back, it MIGHT be a sign that he hadn't heard Miranda's outrageous lie . . . YET.

But I couldn't look over at him. I was **TOO SCARED.** What if he were to say, "I don't talk to girls who cheat in school"?

I WOULD DIE!!!!

I thought about saying hi to Ian and Zoey. They were always nice to me. But what if they didn't trust me either? What if they said, "Don't come to anymore of our academic matches—we only want HONEST supporters"? **UGH.**

And with Valentine's Day just a few weeks away, I can TOTALLY FORGET about getting flowers or candy from ANYONE. Scratch that. The whole class will probably get me a box of those jelly beans that taste like vomit. Yeah, that's what they'll do.

So I just sat quietly at my desk and listened to Mrs. Bristow start the new unit on Europe. She pointed to England on the world map and said we'd study that country first. I usually LOVED learning about different countries, but today I could barely concentrate. I felt a little better when Sophie passed me a note that said, "STOP freaking out. It's going to be OK."

I was SO RELIEVED when the bell finally rang so I could talk to Sophie in the hall.

Catie: That was the worst class ever. What if Miranda's made up even more stuff about me? Who knows what she'll say next! Everyone in class probably hates me now.

Sophie: NO ONE hates you! Well, uh, Miranda might, but WHO CARES. She is definitely one of those MEAN GIRLS like you see on TV. I'm just glad she doesn't come to our academic matches. There's no telling what she'd do.

Sophie even tried to talk me into telling Mrs. Bristow about it. But the LAST thing I want is to act like a tattle-tale. Not only would my friends think I was a cheater, they'd say I act like a second-grader too.

NO THANKS.

But if Miranda keeps it up, she'll give me NO CHOICE but to talk to Mrs. Bristow. And since we have another quiz coming up, I have to make DOUBLE SURE that Miranda doesn't do the same thing again.

I barely spoke to anyone except Sophie for the rest of the day. Matt and Lauren even asked Sophie if I was sick. If only I could say, "Yeah, I'm SICK of Miranda Maroni!"

But I didn't.

I tried to remember the whole turn-the-other-cheek thing.

SOOOOO HAAAARRRRRDDDDD!!!!!!!!!

I could hardly wait to get home and hide in my bedroom. With all the drama Miranda started, I NEEDED A BREAK!

THEN IT HIT ME: I'm supposed to help Josh after school—TOMORROW!

OH MY GOSH!!!!!

I immediately went to my closet and started looking through my clothes.

But WHAT IF JOSH DOESN'T WANT MY HELP NOW?

After all, who would want help from a cheater (WHO'S NOT EVEN A CHEATER TO BEGIN WITH!)? ☹☹

ARGGGGHHHH . . .

I was SOOOO confused.

I messaged Sophie . . . but no answer.

Instead of picking out an outfit or EVEN sketching one on paper, I flopped down onto my bed and cried.

And cried some more . . .

I also prayed to God:

Why do I have to be the one to get picked on? The one class where I actually feel a little smart, and Miranda the Mouth messes everything up. Because of her I feel like everyone is against me. I don't even want to go to school tomorrow. Yeah, I just said that—even if I'm supposed to help Josh Henderson. I'm sorry, God, but I don't want to.

I ended up turning to one of my favorite Bible verses, Philippians 4:6.

"Don't worry about anything, but in everything, through prayer and petition with thanksgiving, let your requests be made known to God."

So that's exactly what I did: I prayed again, thanked God for Jesus and the many blessings He's given me. I also asked Him to give me strength so that I can go to school tomorrow, talk to my friends like normal, and overlook Miranda—no matter what she might say.

GOTTA GO. I just heard the Germ run through the house screaming loud enough to break my window.

UGH.

Who knows what my crazy brother has done this time!

WEDNESDAY, JANUARY 29

Okay, so I really don't even know how to explain what happened at my house yesterday. It was like everything happened in SLOOOOOW MOTION. . . .

Of course, I shouldn't have been surprised that it would have something to do with my brother and that ridiculous cricket-eating reptile. ☹

The Germ had decided that he hadn't been spending enough time with Rosey. He actually said he could tell that her feelings were hurt and she was slightly depressed. **(INSANE!)**

Sooooooo they hung out together on the sofa, watching the usual—Animal Planet.

WELLLLLL, what he didn't know was while they were glued to the TV watching *Land of the Lizards*, the one he was pet-sitting had ESCAPED FROM ITS CAGE.

The Germ didn't even notice Binky was missing until he went to his room to get Rosey's brush. **THEN MY BROTHER WENT BONKERS.**

"CALL 9-1-1! CALL 9-1-1! HELP! HELP! BINKY HAS LEFT THE BUILDING! BINKY HAS LEFT THE BUILDING!" The GERM flew through the house like a maniac. He ran into my room, slinging my sketchbooks left and right, messing up my fashion fabrics, and even looking under my Bible!

"Hey, do you REALLY think that lizard can crawl underneath my Bible? Are you kidding?" I asked.

I really think the Germ lost his mind for a few minutes.

"We have to look EVERYWHERE!" he screamed. "Is there a hole in that sewing machine of yours where he could hide? Huh? Huh? Is there? Is there?"

The Germ then proceeded to look under my bed and even in MY CLOSET! What a drama king!

But the more I thought about the possibility of that reptile being anywhere NEAR ME, I got scared too!

What if I fall asleep and wake up with its tail across my face? I still have nightmares about Rosey's incident.

I decided to help my brother look for Binky.

So did Mom and Dad. They looked under the refrigerator, behind the sofa, and even in the toilet.

No luck.

And no Binky.

That's when the Germ decided to go OUTSIDE and look for him there too.

BAD DECISION.

I MEAN REALLY BAD DECISION.

Before Mom, Dad, or I knew what was happening, my crazy brother had climbed up the biggest oak tree in our yard and crawled out onto one of the branches.

What was he thinking?

Just as I heard him say, "Here Binky Binky . . . where are youuuuuu?", the branch BROKE.

Yes, that's what I said.

It broke . . .

and fell to the ground . . .

with the Germ. . . .

BOOM. ☹

The rest of the night was like **ONE BAD DREAM.**

My brother wasn't knocked out, but he was crying HARD. All that I could understand him saying in between the moaning was *"My leg—it hurts—so bad! I'm scared. . . ."* And then even more crying.

Mom and Dad slowly picked him up and put him into the van. Then Dad drove like a **WILD MAN** to the hospital. I kept my eyes closed and prayed the entire way. I prayed the Germ wasn't badly hurt, and I prayed that we'd all make it to the hospital in ONE PIECE!

After waiting what seemed like a gazillion hours to see the doctor, we finally found out that the Germ's left leg is **BROKEN.**

OUCH.

He said it was only broken in one spot (his tibia, whatever that is), but it would take quite a while to heal. The nurse wrapped the Germ's leg in a big blue cast from his toes to his knee.

He looked miserable. ☹ ☹ ☹

Mom stayed overnight in the hospital with him, and Dad and I drove home.

I still can't believe it happened.

Of course, before Dad and I left the hospital, the Germ asked **ME** to find Binky and take care of Rosey.

GRRRRRRR . . .

Dad and I didn't get home until midnight, and I was already EXHAUSTED.

I looked for that lizard until 2:00 AM.

BUT NO LUCK. ☹

I couldn't sleep a wink, knowing that bearded-disaster dragon was still on the loose.

What if Binky was cuddled up in my silver sequin fabric and stared at me all night long? What if bearded dragons like a little bling too?

Since I'd had such a terrible night, Dad decided to let me stay home from school. He promised to look for Binky and let me get a little more sleep.

YES!!!!! MY DAD IS AWESOME!

But just as I was drifting back to sleep and celebrating that I didn't have to go to school this morning, I suddenly remembered something: I WAS SUPPOSED TO GO TO MRS. BRISTOW'S TUTORING CLASS AND HELP JOSH THIS AFTERNOON!

I TOTALLY FORGOT ABOUT IT!!!!!

ARGHHHHH!!!!!

I bolted out of the bed and explained to Dad that I suddenly didn't feel very tired. I even did a few jumping jacks to prove my point.

But it was no use.

"Catie, we've all had a rough night, and you need to rest," Dad said. "We have to pick up your brother and Mom from the hospital, and unfortunately your Mom has to work this afternoon. You'll have to help with your brother today. I have a big deadline to meet, so I'm counting on you to be a mature young lady."

I CANNOT BELIEVE THIS.

WHY ME???

WHY? why?

WHY?

WHY why?

I didn't have time to message Sophie last night and explain all about the lizard and leg drama. Oh, how I WISHED I could get caught up with her ASAP. I needed SOMEONE to understand. ☹

But Sophie was at school . . . and I wasn't.

I had NO CHOICE but to face REALITY:

1. I'm NOT showing up for Mrs. Bristow's tutoring session, so I won't see Josh or Sophie, and no one will know why!

2. Josh will think I didn't show up because I cheated on the last quiz and was too afraid to admit it!
3. Miranda will offer to help Josh instead—even though she doesn't know ENGLAND FROM ETHIOPIA on a map!
4. I have to spend the rest of the day being the Germ's little servant.

MY LIFE IS SOOOO MESSED UP!!!!

Why does this stuff always happen to me??

Well, I guess there's one bit of good news: Dad found Binky. And guess where he was?

IN THE GERM'S ROOM. ☹

That lazy lizard was stretched out on the window ledge basking in the sun, acting like nothing had happened.

Why hadn't my brother looked there before going all Tarzan on us in the front yard?

At least he'll be relieved that Dad found Binky. THANK YOU, GOD!

I'll admit it would have been HORRIBLE if Dylan's family had come home from China only to find that the pet the Germ was SUPPOSED to be sitting was now the pet that was suddenly MISSING.

WHEW.

If only I could have messaged Sophie, but she wasn't home from school yet. So I decided to sew something . . . anything. I had a purse idea that had been floating around in my head for days. Luckily, my silver fabric hadn't been contaminated by BINKY! ☺

But just as I was threading the needle of my sewing machine, Dad said we had to go pick up the Germ.

Grrrrr . . .

More later. Maybe I'll get to work on my design within the next YEAR!

It took forever to sign all of the paperwork so the Germ could be released from the hospital. They even rolled him out to the van in a wheelchair. I did feel sort of sorry for him. SORT OF.

But my brother is already treated like the baby of the family that he is. He gets his way on everything. NOW it's going to be 100 times worse!

Scratch that—100,000 times WORSE!

Mom and Dad propped him up in front of the TV, covered him up with a blanket, and even put Rosey beside him on the sofa.

UGH. YOU'VE GOT TO BE KIDDING ME!

I gotta pray about this.

I know it's not the right way to feel about my brother. I should be thankful he didn't break both legs . . . or an arm . . . or have a concussion.

I need to ask God for forgiveness—a definite MUST DO.

At least the Germ FINALLY told Mom and Dad that he wants to give part of his allowance, like I am, to help sponsor a child.

"Maybe there are other kids in other countries who fall out of trees too," he told Mom. "They could probably use some help buying medicine or getting a new wrap for their cast or something."

Did I just hear what I think I did? Maybe my brother was delirious from the medicine. He actually sounded . . . well, . . . NICE.

Mom and Dad brought over the laptop, and we all sat on the sofa and looked at the Compassion International website.

There were kids from everywhere in the world: Peru, India, Ecuador, Rwanda, and Haiti. Many were from countries I'd never even heard of.

How could we pick just one kid?

After looking for over an hour on the website, we decided to sponsor a girl from India named Preema! I told Mom that I already knew a little about that country from my social studies class, so I couldn't wait to learn more. Dad filled out all of the information on the website and then got an e-mail saying we'd get more paperwork AND a photograph in the mail—SOON!

SWEET!

But there were soooo many kids on that website. There has to be something else we can do. Evidently the Germ was actually thinking the same thing.

"Dad, can we sponsor more than one kid?" my brother asked. "These kids really REALLY need our help. It makes me sad that we can't help more."

WEIRD. I can't believe that I actually agree with my brother about something!

I DO NOT GET HIM. One minute I want to give him a mushy hug, and the next minute he makes me want to scream!

Sophie always reminds me of **Ephesians 4:32** whenever I'm upset with Miranda. I think I need to read it again and remind myself that it applies to brothers too.

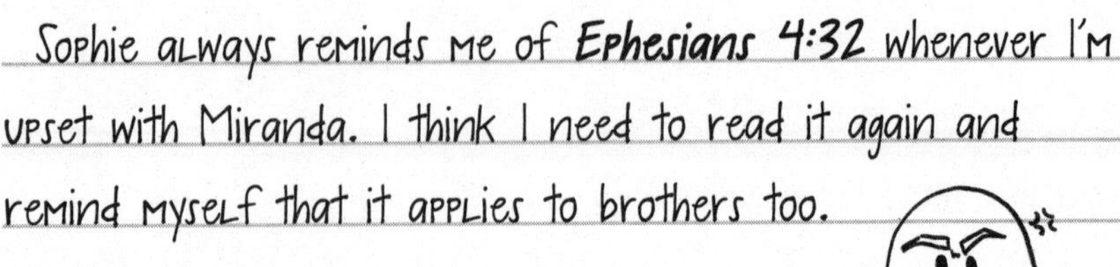

"And be kind and compassionate to one another, forgiving one another, just as God also forgave you in Christ."

—Ephesians 4:32

THURSDAY, JANUARY 30

I am SO READY to go to school today!!! Even though I dread facing Josh and explaining why I wasn't at the tutoring session, I was anxious to talk to Sophie. I still hadn't had time to call or message her. Let's just say I was PREOCCUPIED last night.

That is, I was preoccupied with waiting on the Germ HAND AND FOOT!

I know God's forgiven me for being jealous of him, and I'm still proud of him for being so nice yesterday. But now I have a SERIOUS PROBLEM:

I. AM. TIRED. OF. BEING. HIS. MAID. ALREADY!!!

If my brother needed something to drink, I HAD TO GET IT. If he needed the TV remote, I HAD TO FIND IT.

Oh, but the worst was this: If Binky needed a cricket, I HAD TO FEED HIM. AND I HAD TO FEED ROSEY TOO. ☹

The Germ kept saying that his leg was still hurting, and Dad said it was important that I act like a caring sister and help.

And TODAY I'll even have to help him with his makeup work. ☹

GRRRRRR . . . I should SO GET PAID FOR DOING THIS!

Remember Ephesians 4:32!

MORE LATER . . . I gotta find Sophie before school and fill her in on everything.

This could take **FOREVER!**

Luckily, Sophie was waiting on me at our lockers this morning. She was also wearing a shirt I'd designed for her last year. Just seeing my BFF in one of my designs made me feel better. ☺ Sophie was even wearing the cross earrings I'd given her at Christmas.

After I filled her in on the disasters at home, I couldn't wait to hear what had happened after school.

Nervous Me: *Please tell me YOU-KNOW-WHO didn't help Josh yesterday.*

Sophie: *Calm down. You're right . . . she didn't. I could tell Josh was looking for you, but he didn't say so. Guess you'll have to explain it to him in class.*

HUH???

I wasn't so sure I could even talk to Josh today, let alone explain my CRAZY LIFE to him. He probably wouldn't believe the whole WEIRD story anyway. I'm sure he still sees me as "the fashion diva who cheats her way through school."

Oh and I'm SURE Miranda reminded him about it ten ZILLION times. ☹ ☹ ☹

When we got to social studies class, Mrs. Bristow was nicer than ever. She noticed on my excuse slip why I'd been absent, and she said, "Please tell your brother we hope he feels better soon. He's lucky to have such a sweet sister to help take care of him."

TALK ABOUT FEELING BAD . . . and guilty. I certainly hadn't acted like a sweet sister. Maybe I'll bake the Germ his favorite cookies this weekend.

BUT. THEN. IT. HAPPENED.

Josh had to walk past my desk to get back to his. Sophie was up front talking to Lauren and Ian about the upcoming academic match. I could tell my secret crush was getting ready to speak to me!

GULP!

"Hey, Catie," he said. "Where were you yesterday? I thought you were staying after school to help me and Sophie?"

It was a simple question.

SIMPLE TO ANYONE BUT ME!

I also noticed that Miranda had turned around in her seat and was waiting to hear what I had to say.

"Uh . . . well . . . I had to stay home with my Dad . . . and . . . uh . . . uh . . ." I could barely get the words out of my mouth.

MY BRAIN WAS TOTALLY FROZEN.

TOTALLY FROZEN!

Where was Sophie when I needed her?

"Is your Dad sick?" Josh asked. (Which is just ANOTHER reason why Josh is so AWESOME—he actually CARES!)

My mouth felt like I'd eaten a whole bag of cotton balls.

"Uh . . . yeah," I said, looking down at my shoes. "Oh, I mean, NO! Dad's okay, but my brother isn't. And I had to . . . uh . . . uh . . ."

I immediately started fiddling with the loose wire in my spiral-bound notebook.

How could I say, "I had to stay home, take care of my brother, look for a bearded dragon, feed my brother's skunk, and, oh yeah, catch crickets because my brother fell out of a tree"?

WHO ON EARTH WOULD BELIEVE THAT?

It sounded as crazy as Miranda's lie!

That's when Miranda just had to act like her typical self. "Catie probably stayed home to make cheat notes for the next quiz," she whispered to Emily. "Or maybe she had a dress to design for Beyoncé or something. HA!"

Miranda said it loud enough for me and the rest of the class to hear her. She knew EXACTLY what she was doing.

That's when I lost it.

"I did NOT!" I stood up and said. "For your information, Miranda, my brother was in the HOSPITAL, thank you very much. LEAVE ME ALONE!"

Miranda just stared at me and rolled her eyes.

So did everyone else.

IT WAS AWFUL. ☹ ☹ ☹

I sat down and shrunk down as low as I could into my seat. But it gets worse.

"Catie, I'd like to see you after class," Mrs. Bristow said. "But for now, you need to be reading your chapter on Spain, just like your classmates are doing. You have a quiz coming up, after all."

I could barely breathe. Why did I open my mouth? What if I got sent to the principal's office? I would be grounded for all of eternity!

Why didn't I just ignore Miranda?

So much for me trying to turn the other cheek. ☹

I couldn't wait to tell Mrs. Bristow the WHOLE STORY. It was time that our teacher knew the REAL Miranda—the LIAR!!

But when I told her all about it after class, Mrs. Bristow DID NOT react how I'd hoped. ☹

Catie: *I'm sorry Mrs. Bristow, but I've just about had it with Miranda. She told everyone that I cheated on the last quiz. That is SO not true! I'm sorry, but she drives me CRAZY!*

Mrs. Bristow: Catie, there's no use shouting at others in front of the class, even though I understand why you'd be upset. I'll talk with Miranda. Remember, sometimes it takes more strength to ignore others than to lash out at them. You just concentrate on how well you're doing in my class. It will all work out in due time.

It drives me crazy when adults say stuff like "it will all work out." Blah, blah, blah . . .

How did my teacher know that? It sure didn't look that way to me. I could hardly wait to go to my locker. If only I could crawl inside it and close the door.

But when I got there, I could tell that Sophie was dying to tell me something. She had the strangest look on her face. . . .

"You MISSED IT," Sophie whispered, motioning me to come closer. "Josh just let Miranda have it. I watched the whole thing go down at her locker."

"What?" I asked. "Why?"

My BFF was making **ZERO SENSE.**

"Josh told Miranda to lay off bothering you, and that everyone knew SHE was the one who was lying," Sophie said. "I couldn't believe it. He just walked right up to her and said that. You should have seen Miranda's face."

WHOA.

I couldn't believe Josh had done that—and for ME! Maybe things were going to work out just as Mrs. Bristow had predicted.

But then, the MOST SHOCKING THING IN THE WORLD HAPPENED:

Sophie said she actually FELT SORRY for Miranda.

HUH??

There's **NO WAY** Sophie could have meant that!

NOT. IN. A. ZILLION. YEARS!!!!!!

Catie: Can you repeat what I think I just heard? It almost sounded like you said, **"I feel sorry for Miranda."**

Sophie: That's what I said. It was nice for Josh to stick up for you, but I wonder how Miranda feels. Don't get me wrong, she shouldn't have said those things. But if I'd lied about someone, caused her to get in trouble in class, and also got chewed out by the cutest boy in middle school—all in one day—I'd feel pretty terrible. It's gotta be tough being Miranda Maroni right now.

I could NOT believe those words had come out of Sophie's mouth! I slammed my locker, said "WHATEVER!" and stomped off down the hall.

Why didn't Sophie feel sorry for ME?

Miranda Maroni deserved EVERYTHING she had coming to her!

SOME KIND OF B.F.F. SOPHIE MARTIN TURNED OUT TO BE. ☹☹

ADD TO PRAYER LIST:

* Pray I can understand WHY my BFF has betrayed HER BFF (that BFF being ME!).

FRIDAY, JANUARY 31

If only Dad would have made me stay home like he did the other day. I was in NO MOOD to go to school.

I was still mad at Sophie.

How dare she feel sorry for Miranda Maroni—*the biggest bully ever!* I still couldn't believe that Sophie—MY BFF—had said those exact words to my face! She even had the nerve to message me on the computer last night.

But I didn't reply back. I was too upset.

Maybe that's why Sophie didn't even speak to me in art today. ☹ And I didn't care if she did. Instead, I tried to concentrate on Mrs. Gibson's talk about Leonardo da Vinci. That guy was a genius, not to mention an amazing artist. I wasn't a fan of his painting *Mona Lisa*, but I really liked *The Last Supper*. There was even a copy of it at our church.

Sophie didn't seem to be listening at all. In fact, she acted a little nervous. But I knew it had nothing to do with me. The academic team was just one match away from the regional championship. They have to beat Davidson Middle School tomorrow, or it's ALL OVER.

Usually before a match, I help Sophie prepare by asking her study questions at lunch.

But not today. ☹

My EX-BEST FRIEND hung out with Ian and Lauren and spent every single minute looking at old study questions with them. I even overheard her laughing.

It was terrible. ☹ ☹ ☹

I sat at lunch all by myself for what seemed like FOREVER. Who would want to sit with me anyway? After all, I was the one who ran her big mouth in front of everyone in class.

My friends probably think I'm a bigger bully than Miranda.

Maybe they're right. What kind of Christian example had I turned out to be? But hadn't Miranda deserved it?

Just as I was about to feel even MORE sorry for myself, YOU-KNOW-WHO came by . . .

Matt was with him, so at least that was good. Matt usually hangs out with Josh, sorta like Sophie hangs out with me . . . or USED TO, that is. ☹

THEN I TOTALLY FREAKED: THEY BOTH SAT DOWN AND ATE LUNCH WITH ME!

Once again, **I FROZE.**

Should I tell Josh that I heard he'd chewed Miranda out yesterday? Do I thank him for sticking up for me?

BUT THE WORDS THAT CAME OUT OF JOSH'S MOUTH SURPRISED ME EVEN MORE.

Awesome Josh: Hey, Catie, why aren't you sitting with Sophie?

Nervous Me: Oh, uh, hi Josh. Well . . . uh . . . Sophie and I sort of had a falling out about something. That something being Miranda.

Even-More-Awesome Josh: Figures. What's Miranda done now? I guess you heard that I got onto her for saying junk about you.

Thankful Me: Yeah, Sophie told me. Thanks, Josh. That was really cool. I'm glad SOMEONE understands how rude Miranda is to me.

Christian Josh: Sooo . . . uh . . . about that. After I told Miranda off, I saw her later crying to Emily about it. It wasn't right that she lied about you, but I shouldn't have chewed her out like that. I apologized to her this morning. Sorry, Catie, but I just don't get you girls. Too much drama. Maybe Miranda will apologize to you one of these days.

WHAT??

I suddenly lost my appetite and couldn't wait to leave the cafeteria.

First Sophie and now Josh?

Luckily I found my diary in my book bag, just in time.

I'm going to keep to myself for the rest of the day.

WHAT WAS WRONG WITH MY FRIENDS???

I CANNOT WAIT TO GO HOME.

Even if going home means being a MAID to my brother, a GROOMER to a skunk, and a FEEDER of a lizard!

Maybe I should switch schools?

Where is God when I need Him?

Why did I write that I was excited about going home?

WHY, WHY, WHY???

The Germ bugged me the ENTIRE EVENING.

And trust me, BUG is the PERFECT word to describe it.

Since some of those dumb crickets had "accidentally" gotten loose in my room (I still wonder if they've all been found), we were now totally out of crickets for Binky.

FINE BY ME! ☺

I'm not sure what the big deal was anyway. We had plenty of fruit and lettuce to feed that crazy thing.

But NOOOOO, the Germ threw a big baby tantrum. "Binky needs his protein, so he HAS to have CRICKETS!" he squealed. "He MUST eat ten per day! If not, then we have to feed him roaches or hornworms! Don't you know anything, Catie?"

Crickets? Roaches? **HORNWORMS?????**

GROSS!!!!!

So I had to call Mom and ask her to stop by the pet store and bring home MORE crickets. And of course, YOU-KNOW-WHO had to put them in the little Styrofoam container, since the Germ couldn't hobble over and do it. ☹

DID I MENTION HOW MUCH I DETEST BUGS???

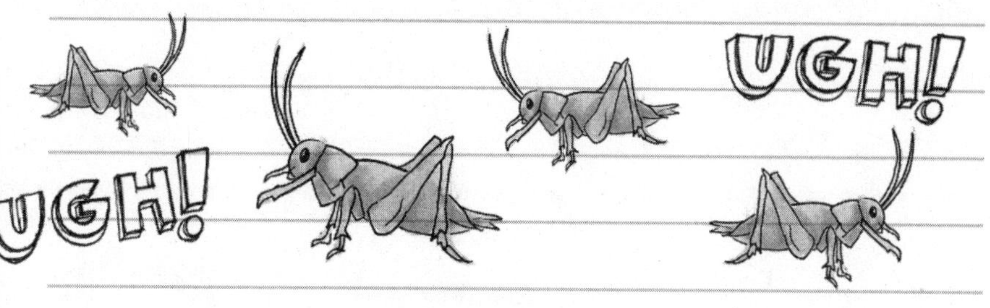

Once all the cricket drama died down, I thought I might get to go to my room and design a few things. Since we're learning about Spain and England in Mrs. Bristow's class, I checked out a book at the library called *Royal Families*.

It would be SO AWESOME to be an actual PRINCESS! Tiaras, diamonds, ball gowns, etc. OOH LA LA! That would be INCREDIBLE!

I'm sure members of the royal family NEVER have to feed their own pets, or anyone else's for that matter. And when it came to school bullies, they probably just lock them away in a dungeon or something.

If only I could be so lucky.

But of course, Josh or Emily would probably bail her out anyway. ☹

Just as I was putting the finishing touches on the sketch for a GORGEOUS green evening gown, the Germ hollered that he needed my help—***AGAIN.***

GRRRRR . . .

This time it had something to do with the computer not working.

I wasn't surprised. Last month the Germ spilled an ENTIRE can of soda on the keyboard. Sparks flew like crazy and Mom even grabbed the fire extinguisher, just in case it went up in flames.

We had to go two weeks without a computer, and I almost went **INSANE!** Even though the guy at the fix-it place

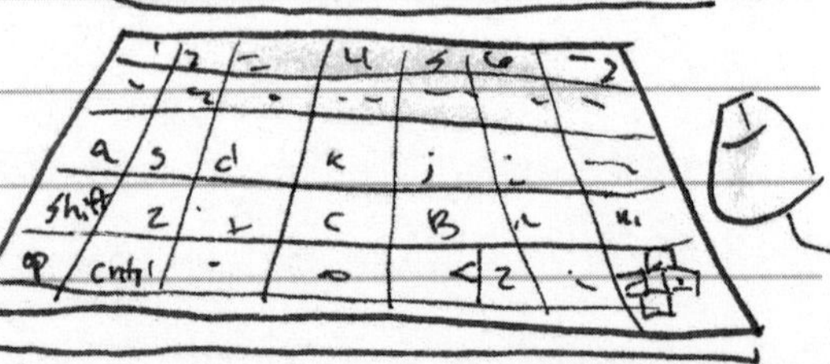

said it was "almost as good as new," I knew it wasn't. The keyboard **STILL STICKS.** ☹

Last week I messaged Sophie about one of my designs. Instead of typing "What do you think?", it typed "Hat o u Hink?"

Sophie thought I'd lost it.

And after all the drama with Miranda this week, I'm sure Sophie's mind hasn't changed. ☹

But the Germ needed help with Skype this time. He acted like it was life or death that he be at the computer at 7:00 P.M. Dylan was going to be on the computer, too, and wanted to see Binky. It was 7:00 A.M. in China, which seemed TOTALLY strange. It was already Saturday over there!

WEIRD.

Not only was the whole time difference thing strange, but the fact that Dylan truly missed that reptile was BONKERS.

It took an eternity to help the Germ get over to Mom's desk. ***THEN*** I had to set up the computer, ***THEN*** I had to go get Binky, and ***THEN*** I had to sit Binky on the Germ's shoulder so Dylan could see him.

RIDICULOUS!

I'll admit, though, it was cool when Dylan's face popped up on the computer screen. I could also see a beautiful Chinese building in the background and wondered where they were exactly. The Germ acted crazy and pressed Binky's face to the screen as close as he could. That lizard probably looked like Godzilla from Dylan's point of view.

"Here he is, Dylan! Here he is!" the Germ said. "I think Binky's even gained a little weight, don't you? Oh, and he and Rosey are the BESTEST FRIENDS EVER! I'm gonna see if Mom will buy me my own bearded lizard after you pick up Binky. I don't want Rosey having any separation anxiety or anything. That's a big problem according to Skunks 101 on the Animal Channel."

OH. MY. GOSH.

DID my brother just say that? And since he's the baby, they'll probably say yes!

PLEEEEEZE GOD, DON'T LET A BEARDED DRAGON BECOME A PERMANENT RESIDENT IN THIS HOUSE!

I overheard Mom ask Dylan's mom how the adoption thing was going. Evidently, the orphanage is just outside Beijing, and they're picking up their new daughter THIS SUNDAY! Then they'll have to stay there one more week and take care of paperwork and stuff.

OH, and HER NAME IS LILY! I LOVE IT!

Dylan's mom said they plan to learn all about the Chinese culture so Lily can appreciate where she came from. How cool is that?

As soon as the call was over, I FINALLY got the chance to get on the computer myself. I decided to read about China on a few websites. They definitely have the yummiest food ever, even though I stink at using chopsticks. I usually end up having to ask for a fork and spoon—ESPECIALLY when it comes to rice.

I had NO IDEA that in many parts of Asia, people can't pray and worship God in public. In some places, people are even put into prison for wanting to learn about Jesus.

WOW.

That didn't make any sense.

Mom said it was true though. In fact, she said there are a ton of countries that don't allow their citizens to worship Jesus openly.

THAT'S HORRIBLE!!

I can't imagine not being able to pray anytime I wanted. I'm sure glad Dylan's little sister is coming to a country where she can learn about Jesus and not have to hide it!

I couldn't wait to message Sophie and tell her that we really needed to pray about this.

But then I suddenly remembered that I was mad at Sophie. ☹

And that I missed her—A LOT.

The more I thought about it, the more I realized I was mad at her and Josh over something totally dumb. They were acting like Christians SHOULD act.

I WASN'T. ☹

I decided to message Sophie. . . .

But no answer.

"Why don't you just call her on the phone?" Dad suggested, after I'd explained to him the whole Miranda drama. "Some things need to be said out loud instead of typed. I'm so glad you realized why your friends acted the way they did."

But when I called Sophie's cell, her Mom answered her phone. ☹

"Oh, hi, Catie! Sophie can't come to the phone right now. She and Lauren are studying for the big match tomorrow. Say a prayer for them. They're going to need it!"

Lauren is hanging out at Sophie's house??

I should have seen this coming.

Sophie's already got a new best friend, . . . and it's a girl who's WAY SMARTER than I'll ever be!

MY LIFE STINKS. ☹☹☹

ADD TO PRAYER LIST:

1. Figure out a way to tolerate my pest of a brother.
2. Pray for Dylan's family in China. (I can't wait to see Lily!)
3. Figure out a way to apologize to Sophie.

SATURDAY, FEBRUARY 1

I'll admit it. . . .

I'M SCARED.

What if Sophie has written me off and has no desire to be friends with me anymore? I'm not so sure I can find a new best friend. There's no other girl in middle school who understands me like Sophie.

I kept checking the computer last night, but there were ZERO messages from her. ☹

When Mom saw me moping around the house this morning, she quickly reminded me of what I needed to do:

Go cheer on the academic team AND apologize to Sophie.

I can't believe I'm admitting it, but Mom's probably right. If I really want to show my BFF I'm sorry, I should go show my support for something that's SUPER important to her.

Come to think of it, Sophie does that for me. She wears the shirt I made for her at Christmas all the time. She's also said the handbag I made for her birthday is her very favorite bag. Sophie knows how much I love fashion, so it's important to her too.

What was I thinking for EVER being mad at Sophie? And why, again, was I mad at Josh? After all, he stuck up for me and told Miranda to lay off. But when he apologized to her later, I should have realized he was acting like Jesus commands us to act.

I had A LOT of apologizing to do and had NO CLUE where to start. It was definitely something to pray about, that's for sure.

More later—I have an academic match to attend and MUST find something to WEAR! ☺☺☺

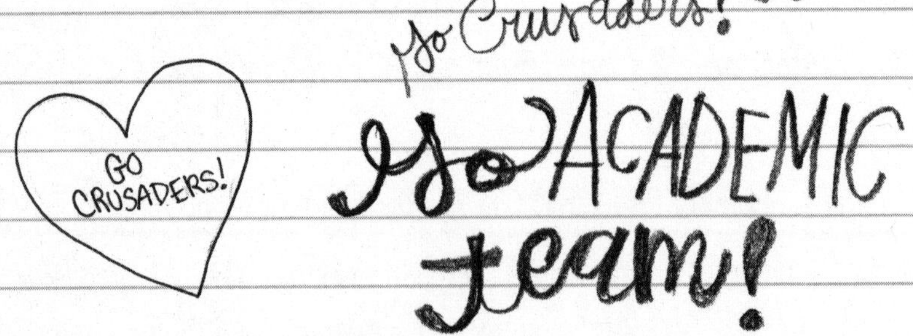

I'm SO GLAD I went to the match. Mom took me early, and luckily Sophie was sitting in one of the auditorium chairs going over her notes.

I had to think fast. The quick recall match was almost ready to start.

Nervous Me: Hey, Soph . . . Uh, I wanted to make sure I came to cheer you guys on. That is, if you don't mind? I'm really sorry that I got mad at you. You were acting like a Christian, and I wasn't. Miranda just makes me crazy. **I hope we're still BFFs?**

Sophie: Of course we are. Duh! It's hard for me to put up with Miranda too. TRUST ME. But I try to remember that I do a TON of stuff wrong, too, and Jesus still loves me. Know what I mean?

Did I ever.

Once again, Sophie was tutoring me in something I stunk at.

I had two HUGE reasons to thank Mom for talking me into attending the match:

1. Sophie and I are BFFs again.
2. I got to see Clairemont Middle School **DOMINATE DAVIDSON!**

Lauren didn't miss a single question about random musical instruments. She knew answers about ones that don't even exist anymore!

Zoey knew the most random facts about the Seven Wonders of the Modern World.

And Ian even answered questions about Shakespeare, someone I am CLUELESS about!

But Sophie, STILL MY BFF, was the **STAR** of the team. From the digestive system to plate tectonics, Sophie got every single science question correct. She knew about microbes, she knew about fungi—she even knew every question about renewable energy. (Note to self: see if Sophie can figure out a way to fix my battery on my cell phone! LOL)

SOPHIE is AMAZING!

Everyone stood up and applauded when the moderator announced that Clairemont Middle was the winner. After our team went over and shook hands with the other team, Sophie ran and gave me a double high five. It sure felt better celebrating with my BFF than being mad at her.

But when I looked around at the audience, I suddenly noticed Josh and Matt were there too.

When had they arrived?

I hadn't spoken to Josh since he sat with me at lunch. I was sure he still remembered how terrible I had acted. . . . ☹

I suddenly felt butterflies in my stomach. . . .

Then I started sweating. . . .

Then the dizziness set in. . . .

Other girls might not understand why Josh is still my crush. After all, he actually apologized and felt sorry for you-know-who. But after thinking and praying about why he did, it secretly made me like him even more. . . .

Josh did the right thing and didn't care if people thought he was cool or not.

LIKE I'VE ALWAYS SAID: **HE'S THE DREAMIEST GUY EVER!**

Principal Martin was so excited about the team victory that he ordered pizza for everyone after the match. And since he's also Sophie's dad, no one thought it was weird when he went up to her and kissed her right on the forehead. Well, Sophie thought it was weird and turned ten shades of pink. LOL!

And get this: while everyone was hanging out, JOSH even got out a piece of pizza for me and said, "Here's a fresh slice for you, Catie."

OH. MY. GOSH!!!!!!

That surely meant he wasn't upset with me! Sophie even looked over and gave me a quick thumbs up. ☺ IT WAS WONDERFUL!

But my BFF turned a ZILLION shades of red just a few minutes later. While everyone was sitting around inhaling slices of cheese pizza, Sophie opened the lid and a grabbed a steaming hot pepperoni slice.

And I do mean STEAMING HOT. Without even thinking about it, she took a ginormous bite and suddenly screamed, **"h . . . h . . . HOT!"** with a mouth full of cheese.

I've never seen a girl throw a piece of pizza down so fast—so fast that a large slab of pepperoni, sauce, and cheese fell—SPLAT—right onto her khaki pants.

OOPS. ☹

I could tell Sophie was TOTALLY embarrassed.

And to make things worse, Miss Turner freaked. She ran over to Sophie with a cloth and screamed, "Get some cold water on that stain, Sophie—and FAST! We've only had these uniforms a few weeks and can't afford to order more pants. It's not in our budget, for goodness sake!"

I wanted to say, "That pepperoni is the best thing that ever happened to those pants."

But I didn't. Josh was sitting there, after all. I needed to be on my best behavior. I didn't want to sound like a fashion diva or anything, but those uniforms DESPERATELY needed some SERIOUS fashion assistance!

Hehehe!

After the pepperoni predicament, I talked Sophie's dad into letting her stay over with me.

I may juuuuussssttttt have a plan. . . .

IF I can try out my ideas on Sophie, and IF Sophie approves, the CMS academic team might be in for a total transformation, courtesy of Catie Conrad . . .

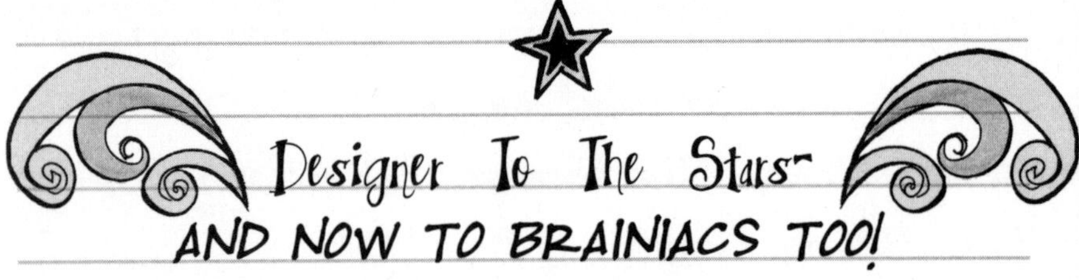

(Seriously, there should be a reality show about this. ☺) Later!

I gotta go find my sketchbook!

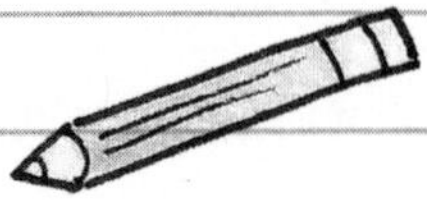

SUNDAY, FEBRUARY 2

Last night was AWESOME! Sophie and I stayed up late, and I came up with some AMAZING sketches for the new team uniforms. We looked online and in magazines for inspiration and then brainstormed our own ideas. I did a zillion sketches using our school colors, and Sophie numbered the ones we liked best from 1 to 5.

After taping them up on the wall, we stood back and studied the sketches, making notes on a few things to change. I felt like a REAL DESIGNER who was creating something magnificent for a client!

But then I HAD TO FACE REALITY. ☹☹☹

Soph reminded me of a few tiny problems:

1. There's no way Ian is going to like what I came up with. He knows I usually just design girl stuff. He is obviously NOT one of those.
2. There's only one academic match left—the regional final—and it's just TWO weeks away! I HAVE TO WORK FAST!
3. Miss Turner already said they have NO MORE MONEY in the school fund, so problems #1 and #2 are pointless anyway. ☹

ME AND MY DUMB IDEAS.

ZERO DOLLARS + ZERO TIME = **THE PLAN OF DOOM.** ☹

This is definitely going to be an unspoken prayer request at Sunday school today. Like Sophie said, "All we can do now is to pray about it and think of how Jesus might handle this." I guess she's right.

Of course, when I think about anything important, I doodle about it in my diary. So this morning my pages are filled with school uniform designs that may NEVER become a reality. ☹ ☹ ☹

GTG. Dad's honking his horn in the car, and I gotta run get my Bible!

CHURCH WAS SO COOL TODAY!

In Sunday school class, Mrs. Childers taught a lesson from Nehemiah 6. How did she know I needed to hear this? She said when Nehemiah planned to rebuild the walls of Jerusalem, tons of people told him he could never do it.

BUT. HE. DID! He just kept on praying to God and worked really hard at it.

Sophie and I instantly thought the same thing. "See, Catie?" Soph whispered, "We need to do just like Nehemiah. Even if we think Ian and Miss Turner might say no to our idea, we can't give up now. We just need to pray and work hard on our plan."

Once again, my BFF was right. ☺

At church, Dad gave everyone an update about Dylan's family in China, and Mom suggested that our church host a small baby shower for them. Some of us are even going to meet them at the airport with posters and everything. It's gonna be SO COOL!

And yours truly will be making the signs! ☺☺☺

On the way home, I asked Mom what she thought about some of us kids doing something for Dylan too. I thought he might get a little jealous of his new sister getting all the attention. I could DEFINITELY relate to that.

Naturally, my brother had to listen in on my conversation with Mom and put in his two cents.

The Germ had a point. He knows Dylan better than I do. I could also tell that my brother REALLY dreads going back to school tomorrow. It will be his first day back since breaking his leg, so I feel a teeny bit sorry for him.

Just a little . . .

But I can't worry about that now. I have to figure out how I'm going to approach Miss Turner about the uniforms. Maybe Mom can give me some advice.

Gotta **STOP** writing and **START** brainstorming!!!!!

Later!!!!!!

If this is how Coco Chanel got started, then COUNT ME OUT!

Designing clothes for me and Sophie is SUPER EASY. But trying to come up with ideas that OTHER people might like—especially Ian—is NEXT TO IMPOSSIBLE!

WHAT WAS I THINKING?

There's no way Miss Turner is going to buy into this. (My chances are better of seeing Taylor Swift wear one of my dresses at the mall!)

And even if these changes aren't huge, IT'S STILL GOING TO COST the team SOME $$$.

The last time I checked, I don't remember a money tree growing on the school football field.

And I can only imagine how Miranda would react if she got a hold of these sketches. I'd probably have to drop out of middle school and go into hiding for the rest of my life!

I have no choice but to talk to Mom about it.

STRESSED-OUT ME: Mom, you should see the CMS academic team uniforms. They're hideous, and no one likes them—especially Sophie! SOMEONE has to do SOMETHING!

TYPICAL MOM: Catie, I know you love fashion, but it's not all about what's on the outside. You know that, right?

DUH ME: Sure I know that, but what if all the kids on the team agree that they NEED a fashion rescue? Those clothes are screaming for help!

SMART MOM: What does Miss Turner think about this? She's in charge, Catie. You need to talk to her about it first.

SUDDENLY DEPRESSED ME: I was afraid you'd say that. I already know what she's going to say, Mom: "We have no money for new uniforms, Catie Conrad." Blah blah blah!

SUPER-BRILLIANT MOM: You need to try and be more

understanding, dear. Money for schools is really tight these days. Remember how tough it's been raising money for different missions at church? How about going through that closet full of fabric in the basement? You have quite a collection. Then maybe the whole cost thing won't be an issue.

O.M.G. ME: That's an AWESOME idea! I forgot about the stuff in the basement! Will you help me? I only have two weeks to give those uniforms some PIZZAZZ!

CAUTIOUS MOM: I'll only help you IF you talk to the academic coach and she gives you permission. That's a big IF. Be prepared. She may not agree to it, and you'll have to respect her wishes. Deal?

AGREEING ME: DEAL. ☹ Oh, and one more thing, do you mind if I mess up the kitchen a little? I thought I'd bake the Germ, er, Jeremy some cookies. You know, to cheer him up a little. Pleeeezeee?

IMPRESSED MOM: That's so sweet of you, Catie. My little designer is turning into a thoughtful young lady.

SHEESH! She didn't have to go THAT far! LOL!

So that's how it all went down.

I have NO MORE TIME to write in my diary!!!!

I HAVE TO:

1. Bake the Germ some snickerdoodle cookies. I know he dreads going back to school tomorrow, so baking his favorite cookies might cheer him up. (I'm REALLY trying to be nice to him, even though I know he won't share the slightest crumb.)
2. Go to the basement and sort through fabric.
3. Come up with a plan that will convince Miss Turner to hear me out.
4. PRAY it works.

MONDAY, FEBRUARY 3

I AM SOOOOO READY FOR TODAY!

At least I think I am. . . .

What if I'm not????

I've been up since 6:00 A.M. putting the final touches on my sketches. Miss Turner is always on hall duty, so I know I'll run into her first thing this morning. I messaged Sophie all about it last night, and she promised she had my back on the whole thing. ☺

I am so blessed to have a friend like Sophie.

I put on extra deodor-ant, just in case I become a nervous wreck and get pit stains during my presentation. That would **STINK** in more ways than one. Wet armpits are most definitely a FASHION DON'T.

I'm not the only one who's nervous this morning.

So is my brother.

The Germ barely even touched those snickerdoodles I baked for him yesterday. **STRANGE.** He usually inhales those things in two seconds.

"Why are you freaking out about going back to school?" I asked him in the van. *"Everyone will feel sorry for you and treat you like a rock star. You'll get to be the first in line at the cafeteria and everything. Or maybe a cute girl will carry your books around for you? Ooohhhhh, you'll LOVE that!"*

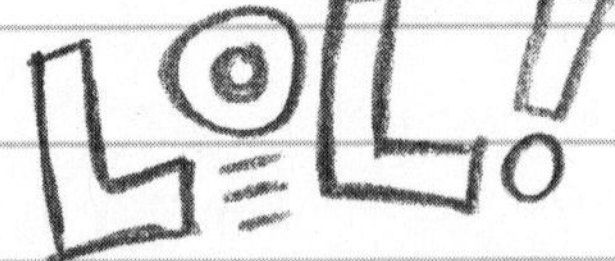

"YOU'RE GROSS, CATIE!" he squealed as Mom helped him out of the van. *"Who wants some YUCKY girl carrying his books? Everyone will probably make even MORE fun of me now!"*

I had no clue what my brother was talking about, but I didn't have time to worry about it. I had a SUPER IMPORTANT presentation to get ready for!

YIKES!!!!

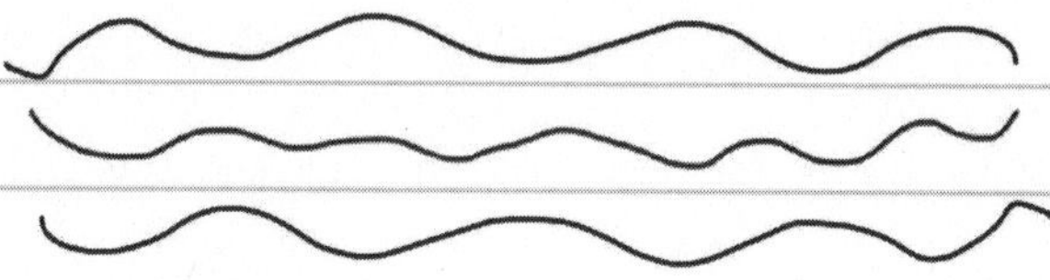

I could hardly make my legs move on my way to the library, Miss Turner's usual duty spot. I even felt a trickle of sweat roll down my arm.

NOT. GOOD.

But I had to keep going.

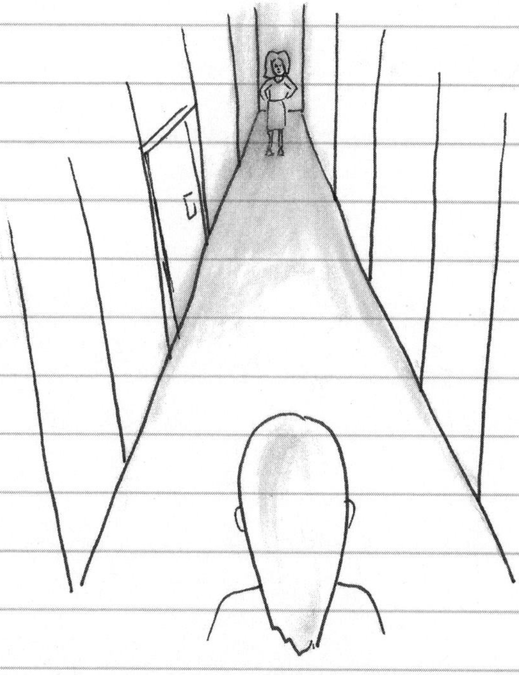

I took a deep breath, got out my sketchbook, and suddenly noticed the BEST THING EVER: Sophie, Zoey, and Lauren were standing there talking to Miss Turner. Even Ian was there!

YES! It was almost like they were WAITING FOR ME.

AMAZING Sophie: Hi, Catie. I was just telling Miss Turner how pumped we are about the regional match. Oh, and I ALSO told her I couldn't get that pizza stain out of my khakis. Bummer—RIGHT?

Freaking-Out Me: Oh, uh, yeah, RIGHT!

Miss Turner: What am I going to do with you kids? You may just have to attend that match in a stained pair of pants, Sophie. Sounds like that's your only option.

AWESOME Zoey: But what if Sophie had ANOTHER OPTION? No disrespect, Miss Turner, but those uniforms are a little boring. It seems like they're missing something.

BRILLIANT Lauren: Yeah, I agree with Zoey. Is there any way we could find some way to give them, you know, a little more style?

I was SPEECHLESS. I couldn't believe that my friends were backing me up like this!

That's when Sophie went for it. "Miss Turner, did you know that Catie is an AMAZING fashion designer? She practically designs stuff in her sleep! Catie, do you think you could help us out?"

I wasn't sure what to say to Sophie since Miss Turner hadn't said much during the whole conversation. "Uh, well, SURE I could!" I said quickly. "That is, uh, if Miss Turner says it's okay."

But I could tell Miss Turner was a little skeptical. "Sophie, I see what you and your friends are trying to do, but like I said on Saturday, we have no available funds. I'm sure that Catie is extremely talented, but we just can't afford it."

THIS WAS MY BIG CHANCE.

"Miss Turner, what if I told you that the team CAN afford it, and that I've found FREE fabric to use?" I asked. "I'd just be altering the uniforms a little—you know—like Lauren said, to give them a little style."

I could barely breathe as I quickly pulled out my sketch-pad and flipped through the sketches. Lauren "ooo-ed," Zoey "ahh-ed," and Sophie said, "Oh, I LOVE THIS!"

Miss Turner studied each sketch and sorta smiled a little. Ian just stood there and sulked. ☹

"Oh, and Ian, here's a design for you too!" I quickly flipped to the back and showed him what I'd come up with. He didn't do backflips, but I think he actually liked my idea. Otherwise he wouldn't have said, "Cool, I could live with that."

YES!!!

"Well, you've definitely outdone yourself, Catie Conrad," said Miss Turner. "But I'm not so sure about it."

HOW COULD SHE NOT BE SURE? But Miss Turner went on to explain that she needed to show my designs to Principal Martin and get his approval. Something about guidelines and "being appropriate."

UGH. This was SUCH a typical teacher response!

MY DAY HAD TAKEN A NOSEDIVE.

As we walked to class, I thanked Lauren, Ian, Zoey, and of course my BFF for sticking up for me. Even though they were brainiacs, they were nice brainiacs.

I'll admit it: I was suddenly jealous that I wasn't on the academic team too. It would be cool to hang out with them more, not to mention dress in matching new uniforms. But based on my conversation with Miss Turner, the uniforms weren't going to happen anyway.

Sophie could tell I was disappointed. "Come on, Catie, it's not like Miss Turner made a final decision or anything.

Maybe she liked them and just didn't know how to tell you."

I guess Soph had a point.

"Chill out. I know I'm sounding like my mom, but try to remember that as long as we're pleasing to God, that's what matters. I'll talk to Dad about it tonight," she said. "Remember, I do have a little influence on the principal."

SWEET! ☺

For some reason I hadn't even thought of that! Hopefully, Sophie can talk her dad into approving my designs. After all, he's the BOSS of the entire school. ☺

This was going to be a good day after all. ☺

OR NOT.

Just as Sophie, Zoey, and I were walking into social studies class, we overheard a big mouth in the back of the room: "Have you heard the latest? I'm not saying any names, but there's ONE GIRL in here that thinks she's going to be the designer for every uniform in the ENTIRE school. All I can say is, NOT GONNA HAPPEN."

I'd know that voice anywhere: **M.M.**

She was standing in the back of the room and talking to Emily—the only girl in school that was crazy enough to put up with her.

"It's not every school uniform," I heard Zoey fire back. "It's the ACADEMIC team uniforms—AND they're gonna be AMAZING, if you ask me!"

WHOA.

"Well I don't remember asking you," Miranda said under her breath. She always seemed to have the last word.

GRRRRR . . . THAT GIRL DRIVES ME BONKERS!!!

"She's just jealous, Catie," Zoey whispered as she walked back to her desk. "Miranda has to BUY style whereas you have it naturally and can create your own ORIGINAL stuff that she doesn't have. Oh well, too bad for her."

I was speechless.

I could hardly concentrate on the review sheet that Mrs. Bristow had handed us. *How could I?* I'd just watched Zoey Franklin—ONE OF THE SMARTEST GIRLS IN MY CLASS—stand up to Miranda Maroni, the rudest girl in middle school.

I wanted to let Miranda have it, too, but then I remembered Mrs. Bristow's little talk with me last week. I also remembered what Josh and Sophie had said about Miranda. **They felt sorry for her.** Sometimes being a Christian and turning the other cheek feels TOTALLY impossible. But I'd seen Sophie do it, . . . and I knew Josh did it too.

Maybe I'll tell Zoey what Sophie and Josh had suggested to me. We've got to help each other when it comes to dealing with girls like M.M.

BUT THEN I JUST REMEMBERED SOMETHING: Zoey told Miranda that their uniforms were "GONNA BE AMAZING."

Mr. Martin REALLY needed to hurry and approve my designs. I had A LOT of cutting and sewing to do! These HAVE to be THE MOST FASHIONABLE UNIFORMS in the history of the entire school.

Maybe Zoey or Sophie will ask me to be the team manager or something? I may not be as smart as they are, but at least I'll be the "official designer" for the CMS academic team—that's WAY more important anyway. ☺

TUESDAY, FEBRUARY 4

I got up this morning and prayed before school. Yeah, that's what I said.

I prayed that Miss Turner got my designs approved, and I also prayed for my little brother. This time it had nothing to do with a stink-infested skunk or a creepy cricket-loving lizard.

No, this was **SERIOUS.** (Unfortunately, I'm experienced at this kind of stuff. ☹)

After hibernating in his room for an eternity last night, the Germ finally came out and explained what had happened at school.

"I TOLD you!" he said to Mom. "When my class found out I'd broken my leg by falling out of a tree, a few of the kids wouldn't quit laughing. Three of them even called me Monkey Boy and asked if I wanted a banana. Please don't make me go back to school, Mom. I don't want to see those boys EVER again!"

Ooooh it made me so MAD. How dare those kids say mean things about my brother? I know I joke around with him a lot, but I'm his SISTER. I'm sure that makes it legal or something.

Mom and Dad were upset, too, but tried to be calm about it. "Jeremy, we really appreciate you telling us about this," Dad said. "If they keep this up, we'll need to talk with your teacher or speak to those boys' parents."

That's when the Germ had a total meltdown. "Please don't say ANYTHING, Dad! That'll just make it worse!" he said. "I'll get used to it. Ever since they realized I know a lot of stuff about animals, they've been giving me a hard time. When Dylan told them about Rosey last year, they even called me Skunk Breath and went around holding their noses. But I'll get used to it."

But I knew he wouldn't.

He should've told Mom and Dad about this last year. He should've told ME about this last year! I'm sure I could have done SOMETHING.

But how could I when I don't even know how to deal with Miranda?

"Oh, they're just being rude," I said, trying to make him feel better. "Those boys probably wouldn't know how to climb a tree if they tried."

"Neither can I," the Germ said, pointing to his cast. "You did see my leg didn't you?"

Oops. Guess that wasn't the right thing to say.

So that's what happened last night. The Germ totally dreads going to school this morning, and I can't say I blame him.

I couldn't even sleep last night because I was really worried about him.

Yes, this is really Catie Conrad writing this. ☺

GTG. I still have to fix my hair, do a few more fashion sketches, and review one last time for the S.S. quiz.

Of course, I have to brace myself for Miranda too. **What else is new?** ☹

Maybe those boys in the Germ's class are related to her. ☹

UGH.

SO GLAD TO GET HOME.

School **STUNK** today for a variety of reasons:

1. NO LUCK WITH MISS TURNER. ☹

I thought since I'd shown her my perfect designs yesterday, she might have gone ahead and met with Principal Martin. I'd even messaged Sophie about it last night. UNFORTUNATELY, her dad hadn't spoken with Miss Turner yet. According to Sophie he'd had several meetings that were "more pressing." **UGH. WHAT COULD BE MORE PRESSING THAN FASHION? GIMME A BREAK.**

2. THE SOCIAL STUDIES QUIZ. ☹

I didn't feel good about it. One part was matching, and I hate those kind of questions. Just one wrong match and you miss a bunch of other questions. IT WAS ALL MIRANDA'S FAULT. How could I concentrate on facts about England and France when the rudest girl in America was trying to destroy my life?

3. LOCKER CATASTROPHE.

I saved the worst for last. I'd tried hard the entire day to forget about what Miranda had said to Zoey. Actually, I was pretty proud of myself for not letting her get to me. I ignored Miranda, just like I'd told the Germ to ignore those rude boys in his class.

NOW HIRING

• Clairemont Middle School Fashion Designer

—DO NOT APPLY IF YOUR NAME IS CATIE CONRAD!

But when Sophie and I went to our lockers at the end of the day, a neon green piece of paper was taped to my door.

I knew it was Miranda.

Or maybe she put Emily up to it. That sounded more like her.

I quickly tore the paper off my locker and crammed it into the trash can. Miranda's little stunt even made Sophie mad.

"Oh, that Miranda just keeps getting funnier and funnier doesn't she? **Not**," Sophie said. "Sorry she's such a bully, Catie. I guess it's just one more reason to pray for her."

Once again, it was easy for Sophie to say.

I still couldn't.

So, yeah, that's how my day went today:

H—O—R—R—I—B—L—E.

I can only hope the Germ's day went better than mine. I was too upset with my own problems to ask him about it on the way home. Maybe I'll feel like it after I take a nap.

Why do I even TRY to take naps after school? ☹ Mom only let me sleep ONE HOUR this afternoon. ☹

What was with her? Mom should know that kids my age need their REST. I'm in a GROWTH SPURT, or at least that's what the pediatrician said at my last visit. But with the little rest that I'm getting, I'll be lucky to be 5 feet tall!

I'll probably even shrink!

Sometimes I have to wake up and help Mom with the laundry or empty the dishwasher. ☹ But I couldn't nap this afternoon because the Germ was doing some kiddie science project and needed my help.

Normally, I would have put a pillow over my head and tried to ignore him, but today was different. How could I ignore a little shrimp pounding on the door and yelling at the top of his lungs?

UGH.

"I need my special science goggles!" he squealed. "Do you have them, Catie? This is going to be SO AWESOME! You can help too!"

"Yeah, I wore them when I had to handle those CRAZY CRICKETS for you!" I reminded him. "A THANK YOU would be nice."

My brother did seem to be in a little better mood, so I decided to ask him about school.

Me: So, did those guys act nicer to you today?

The Germ: They're NEVER nice to me. I wish Dylan would hurry back. He's the only one that understands.

That's when I decided to tell my brother about Miranda. He even put down his digging tools and really listened.

"Instead of being mad at those boys, maybe you should feel sorry for them," I said.

The Germ looked as confused as I did when Sophie gave me that advice last week.

So I told him what I'd read in Matthew—that God blesses those who are merciful, and that's how I try to deal with Miranda. I also mentioned that Sophie and I even pray for her and that maybe he could do that too.

I wasn't sure if I'd helped my brother or not, but it was a good reminder for me on why I should put up with Miranda—ESPECIALLY after the locker incident.

I was so glad the Holy Spirit had led me to read Matthew chapter 5 last night. Now I knew why. ☺

NOTE TO SELF!

PRAY for strength for my brother, PRAY for those mean boys in his class, and PRAY that I passed that social studies quiz!

Oh, and, uh, pray for Miranda. . . . I guess.

WEDNESDAY, FEBRUARY 5

Still no word from Miss Turner about the uniforms. ☹ What was taking so long???

But GOD must have heard my prayers about the social studies quiz!

When Mrs. Bristow handed back our quiz papers, I almost PASSED OUT when I saw a BEAUTIFUL 92% B+ written at the top. ☺ ☺ ☺

YES!

OH YEAH! OH YEAH!

I was almost sure that I'd failed it. But I'd only missed two of the matching questions about England, and the rest of the quiz was a PERFECT SCORE.

Mrs. Bristow announced that Josh had received the highest in the class with a 104% A++. He'd even answered both bonus questions correctly! I guess that tutoring session with Mrs. Bristow must have helped—even if I hadn't been able to be there. ☹ I'm glad Josh did great on the quiz, but I'm sorta hoping he'll need my help again.

If only I could have ONE MORE CHANCE to hang out with him after class. This time I'll make sure to be there, that is, if my brother DOESN'T lose another creature or go on a wild rescue mission.

Sophie was also smiling big time. She'd brought up her grade with a 97% A, instead of a B like on the last quiz. Maybe her mom will ease up on her a little.

But Miranda didn't look too happy. When she turned around to talk to Emily, I noticed that she'd received a 54% on the quiz—an F. No wonder she was so quiet in class. I'll bet she wished she could be as smart as Sophie today.

Maybe she'll THINK the next time she makes fun of my BFF for being on the academic team!

I'll admit it. I was glad that Miranda had failed.

It served her right since she'd spread a lie about me, taped mean stuff onto my locker, and was even rude to my friends. She deserved what was coming to her.

But deep down, the more I sat in class and thought about it, the more I knew it wasn't right to feel that way about her—even if she was rude.

A few nights ago, Dad read **ROMANS 12:17** to the Germ and me. Paul told the Romans to never try and repay evil with evil and to always try and be honorable like Jesus. I have a feeling that being glad Miranda flunked a quiz was NOT what Paul had in mind.

Come to think of it, I really needed to work on being more honorable at home too. I'm often rude to my brother, complain when I have to help Mom around the house, and occasionally sneak and watch TV shows that my parents say are off limits.

Sometimes I just feel like giving up. Why would Jesus want to love someone as messed up as I am?

Oh No.

But I do think God heard my prayers for the Germ. He just came home and said he'd decided to ignore those boys the entire day. YAY FOR HIM! And I had to CRACK UP when he told me he'd taken a bunch of bananas to lunch. He actually said, "If you're gonna call me Monkey Boy, then I guess you'd like a banana. Here you go." LOLOL!!!! WAY TO GO, GERM!

He said those boys never said a mean word to him the rest of the day. YAY!!!!

GTG, since I have something SUPER IMPORTANT to do.

They've started a youth group at church, and we meet TONIGHT! Pastor Steven seems like the COOLEST pastor ever. He organizes mission trips, pool parties, and even hosts crazy game nights at church. I CANNOT WAIT!

Sophie heard he's also designing T-shirts for the group. Of course, she knew I'd be ALL OVER that! LOL. I hope they're pink . . . or a basic black would be chic too. ☺ I can't believe that I'm admitting this, but I don't care what they look like—I just want to be part of this group!

Sophie, Josh, and Tyler said they were going tonight too. ☺

I have NO IDEA what to wear or how to fix my hair or anything! After all, I have to LOOK PERFECT if my secret crush is going to be there too. ☺ ☺

GOTTA GO!!!

L8R!!!

OH. MY. GOSH.

OUR YOUTH GROUP IS THE BEST! It's called A.C.E., which stands for "Accepting Christ Everyday."

And the red T-shirts are SWEET. Pastor Steven created the coolest A.C.E. logo for the front, and on the back it says "Totally HIS." Sophie and I are wearing ours to school tomorrow with skinny jeans and ballet flats. I'm sure Miranda will have something RUDE to say about it. ☹

After we had hot dogs and the most chocolatey brownies on the planet, Pastor Steven delivered a message based on **Romans 5:8**—"But God proves His own love for us in that while we were still sinners, Christ died for us!"

WOW. So even though I totally mess up sometimes, God still loves me. He doesn't expect me to be perfect because He already knows we sin. DUH. That's why He sent Jesus.

What was I thinking trying to look perfect for Josh tonight?

How CRAZY! The only person I need to try to please is GOD, and He loves me even though I MESS UP TONS OF TIMES!

THANK YOU, GOD. ☺

GTG read my Bible. Pastor Steven says we can't know God if we don't know His Word.

Maybe I'll get Miss Turner's decision about the uniforms tomorrow?

THURSDAY, FEBRUARY 6

School was AWESOME TODAY!

Sophie and I wore our A.C.E. shirts like we'd planned. ☺ My BFF decided to wear tall brown boots as part of her look, and it was so City Chic! She had a leopard print scarf in her hair and gold loop earrings. She is great at accessorizing! ☺

My look was a little different. I'd saved up my allowance and found an AMAZING pair of red ballet flats on sale at the mall last month. 75% OFF!!!! This was my first time wearing them, and I must admit: I am in LOVE with these shoes! I'm almost positive that girls in Paris wear shoes like this. Of course, Mom and Dad thought I was crazy wearing them without socks in the middle of winter, but that would have RUINED the look. Who cares if my feet freeze a little when my look is so EN VOGUE! (BTW, that sorta means "fashionable" in French!)

The perfect red T-shirt + skinny jeans + silver dangle earrings + charm bracelet + RED shoes = FASHION DIVA AWESOMENESS!!!

But, OF COURSE, Miranda didn't think so.

As soon as I stepped foot into first period class, I overheard her say to Emily, "Check out the clown shoes on Conrad today. Wow. There must be a circus in town."

UGH.

WHO DOES SHE THINK SHE IS?

Miranda thinks that because she has a closetful of expensive clothes, she is THE authority on fashion. NOT.

Even though I should care less what Miranda Maroni thinks of me, she still DRIVES ME CRAZY—although not as much as last week. ☺ I kept trying to remember what Pastor Steven mentioned last night. As long as we're pleasing to God, that's ALL that matters.

Despite Miranda's rudeness, several of my friends noticed my shirt and asked what A.C.E. stood for. ☺ That made it super easy to explain, and I even invited them to come to the meetings with me. But a few of the girls said they didn't go to church and doubted their parents would even take them. WOW. **THAT STINKS.** I can't imagine having parents who refused to take me to church.

Maybe that was Miranda's problem too?

I also spoke with Miss Turner right after school. She said she HOPED to have an answer about the uniforms for me **TOMORROW**. FINALLY! EEEEEK!!!!

Luckily I've already started working on them at home since the regional championship is less than two weeks away. A designer must ALWAYS be ready at a moment's notice. ☺

Oh, the COOLEST thing happened after dinner tonight. We received a huge envelope full of info from Compassion International. FINALLY!

COMPASSION INT'L.

I had to practically push the Germ out of the way so I could open it first. Inside was a photograph of Preema dressed in a pretty floral dress, as well as a card that said **"GOD BLESS YOU FOR HELPING ME."** She'd even drawn a picture of a house with flowers on the back of the card. I quickly used a magnet and stuck it on the refrigerator as a reminder to pray for her. My new "sister" liked to draw too. NICE!

According to the information sheet, Preema is seven years old and lives in an orphanage near New Delhi. Her health is good, but she has trouble with her eyesight and needs glasses.

I noticed that she wasn't smiling in the picture, which made me sort of sad. ☹ But I don't blame her. If I had trouble seeing what I was sketching, I'd be upset too. Talk about a TOTAL BUMMER.

I really needed to give Dad more of my allowance to help with Preema and the glasses she needs.

I soooo don't need any more new clothes or shoes. (I CAN'T BELIEVE I JUST WROTE THAT!) Hopefully I can talk the Germ into giving more of his allowance too.

But unfortunately he's too wrapped up with that dingbat dragon to worry about anything else. I just witnessed him in the kitchen fixing Binky a salad and misting his skin with water every other second. UGH.

"Dylan's coming home in THREE DAYS! I have to make sure Binky is looking his absolute best!"

Yes, I love my brother, but sometimes he is ONE WEIRD KID.

At least he's getting around better with his cast and can take care of those crazy pets himself. **THANK YOU, GOD!**

I STILL have nightmares from feeding those creatures last week!

FRIDAY, FEBRUARY 7

I don't have time to write much before school, but I had to mention that TODAY'S THE DAY! I didn't even bug Sophie about it last night because I'm 99% positive of the answer: Miss Turner is going to give me the go-ahead to make the academic uniforms!

I just said another prayer about it, too, just to make sure God heard me correctly.

GTG! FOR ONCE, I CAN'T WAIT TO GET TO SCHOOL!

I can't believe it.

I. CANNOT. BELIEVE. IT.

Miss Turner turned me down.

She turned me DOWN!!!

ACCORDING TO HER:

1. The skirts I designed for the girls are too short. (She even pointed out the dress code in the student handbook!)
2. Even though I offered to use some of my own fabric from home, Principal Martin suggested that Miss Turner "wait and revisit the issue" when they have more funds available.

I knew what that meant: **NOT GONNA HAPPEN.** Just like Miranda had predicted.

Why didn't God answer my prayers about this? It was super important to me, and He knew that!

When word gets out that the new uniforms are a no-go, I'll be laughed out of middle school. It'll only take about two seconds for Miranda to post another sign on my locker. This time, it will say "TOLD YA-LOSER!" What little popularity I have left will be TOTALLY OUT THE WINDOW. ☹

I was also a little ticked off with Sophie. My BFF'S dad is the school principal, and he STILL SAID NO!

I thought Sophie had my back on this?

When I told her and Zoey the news, I tried my best to act like it was no big deal. TRIED, I repeat. But Sophie could tell I was a little upset with her.

UPSET (but secretly mad) ME: Yeah, it's a bummer that your Dad said no. I guess you're stuck with pizza stains and a BORING ol' white shirt.

FEELING-BAD SOPHIE: Guess so. I'm really sorry, Catie. I can't tell my dad what to do. I know he's been really stressed out about the school budget lately. We'll just have to be thankful for what we have, I guess. Am I still invited for that sleepover? I'm looking forward to our spa night.

I'd forgotten all about it. Sophie was supposed to come home with me after school and spend the night. I wanted to say, "No, spa night is CANCELED. You were **supposed** to have my back on this whole thing, and now I can't even count on my BFF! Oh, and your dad doesn't know the first thing about fashion!"

But I didn't say that.

I knew that would have been DUMB, not to mention rude. Sophie was right. She couldn't tell her dad what to do. And I don't want to be the type of friend who's only friends with someone when things are going my way.

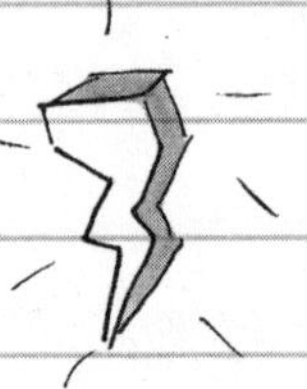

Come to think of it, I probably shouldn't have acted like a know-it-all about fashions or called their white shirts boring either.

The LAST person I want to act like is Miranda Maroni. Being so wrapped up in outward appearance and demanding I get my way sounds more like HER than me.

NOT GOOD.

So I said, "Sure, Soph, it's still on. And Zoey, you're invited to the sleepover too." I also invited Lauren, but she couldn't come because of piano practice.

Pastor Steven would be proud of me for remembering what he'd said at the A.C.E. meeting. More importantly, I know God is pleased. I still didn't understand why He didn't answer my prayers about designing the uniforms, but still, I have to trust Him. I was beginning to be okay with that. ☺

By lunchtime, I'd finally come around to accepting Miss Turner's decision. If they HAD approved my designs, I probably would have run out of time to finish them anyway.

Maybe it was a blessing in disguise. Friday was turning out to be fantastic after all. ☺

That is, UNTIL I went to art class.

Today my favorite class **TOTALLY STUNK!** ☹

Mrs. Gibson decided to do a big Valentine's Day Countdown and was super excited about it. ☹ Taped up on the wall was a swirly red number 7 painted onto a white piece of paper. I DID NOT LIKE being reminded that "you-know-what" was just ONE WEEK away.

7 days away!

YIKES

UGH.

Sophie and I TOTALLY FREAKED when Mrs. Gibson said, "Valentine's Day should be used as a time to show kindness. It's also a day to tell others WE LOVE THEM."

SHE SAID THOSE VERY WORDS!!!!!

My face turned hot pink, and my heart started racing.

I looked over at Sophie and rolled my eyes. I'm sure she was thinking exactly what I was thinking: I still have the **BIGGEST CRUSH EVER** on **J.H.** I'm not sure if it's *love*, but it sure feels like it!

I tried to glance over and check out his reaction to what Mrs. Gibson had said. . . .

NOTHING.
ZILCH.

Josh let all that stuff about LOVE go through one ear and out the other.

Ugh.

I DO NOT UNDERSTAND BOYS.

Oh, and on top of everything else, Mrs. Gibson handed us a GINORMOUS list of art terms to look up and memorize by Monday. ☹

What was she thinking? Who needs to know the difference between a tertiary color and a complementary color? I'm a FASHION DESIGNER, for goodness sake!

I know how to put colors together.

DUH.

I need to CREATE ART, not study a bunch of boring definitions.

But I probably would have been dangerous with a paint-brush today. I was in such a bad mood that there's no telling what I would have painted.

Obviously, Mrs. Gibson had forgotten that today was FRIDAY.

I have way more important things to do:

1. Host SPA NIGHT with Sophie and Zoey.
2. Help Mom decorate at church for the surprise baby shower.
3. Go meet Dylan's family with his new baby sister at the airport. (AND TAKE BACK BINKY!)

I'm especially excited about the last part. ☺

Later!

SATURDAY, FEBRUARY 8

Although there were a FEW minor problems (his name starts with a G and ends with an M), our spa night was AWESOME.

We soaked our feet in Mom's big bathtub then lathered peppermint lotion on our legs and painted our toenails. Zoey used a bright purple polish on her toes, and Sophie used a funky neon yellow on hers. That girl's feet practically glowed in the dark!

We also tried all kinds of facial and wrinkle creams. I know, I know, I don't have any wrinkles—YET. But a girl can never start too soon. **LOL!** The cosmetic lady at the mall gave Mom a ton of samples last week, so Mom gave them all to

us. From scrubs to gels to clay masks, we had every problem covered that could possibly happen to a face. Honestly, I'm not sure if any of that stuff really works, but they sure smell yummy—sorta like roses, lemons, and cucumbers all rolled into one.

After our facials, we ate chocolate chip cookies and got online and looked at hairstyles. Sophie and Zoey had brought over a bunch of hair clips, and I heated up my flatiron and the curling iron that makes corkscrew curls. I looked HILARIOUS after Sophie tried rolling my hair and spraying it with this stuff called Freeze It.

It was more like GLUE IT.

My hair was so sticky that my fingers literally got stuck when I tried to pin part of it back with a hair clip! It took THREE shampoo rinses to wash that junk out. I think Sophie felt the same way about her hair. She tried using my flat-iron and it was WAAAAY TOO FLAT.

I think there's a reason why God gave me my hair and Sophie hers. We looked waaaaay better just letting our hair do its own thing.

Zoey's hair, on the other hand, looked AMAZING. Sophie and I did the coolest braid down the back of her head after watching a YouTube video. Zoey loved it and even sprayed her braid with that Freeze It stuff so it wouldn't move before academic practice.

Zoey also wanted us to watch a new video by a rap artist that her older sister listened to. She said everyone had seen it, and we should check it out too. But I knew about that singer from overhearing some of the kids at school talk about him. He cursed a lot in his lyrics and talked about sex and stuff. Even though it was hard to do, I told Zoey I'd rather not watch it.

"It's just a few curse words," she said. "We'll even turn down the volume on that part." For a second, I thought to myself that Zoey might have a point. Just taking a quick glance shouldn't hurt anything.

Thankfully, Sophie backed me up. "Sorry, Zoey. We're so glad you're at our spa night, but turning down the volume really won't change that video. That's kinda like saying that chocolate chip cookie has poison in it so we'll just eat around the bad part. It's still poison. See what I mean? I don't think we'd be honoring God by watching that stuff."

Why didn't I think of saying something like that?

BUT. THEN. THE. TROUBLE. HAPPENED.

And by t-r-o-u-b-l-e, I mean J-E-R-E-M-Y C-O-N-R-A-D . . . aka: THE GERM.

My eight-year-old brother couldn't resist crashing our GIRLS ONLY spa night! Oh, and not just HIM—he wanted ROSEY and BINKY to get polished and pampered too.

While we were trying out different hairstyles in my bedroom, the PEST sneaked into the bathroom, took Sophie's yellow polish, and PAINTED ROSEY'S TOENAILS!

The Germ seriously painted those creepy little claws on that ridiculous black-and-white fur ball!

Oh, but that's not all: I stopped him JUST IN TIME from doing something EVEN WORSE. He was getting ready to use **MY hairbrush** and **MY spray-n-shine** on Rosey's tail.

He was going to use my HAIRBRUSH– **I repeat, MY HAIRBRUSH**–on that SKUNK's tail without even telling me!

Talk about sneaky–and the **NASTIEST THING OF ALL TIME!**

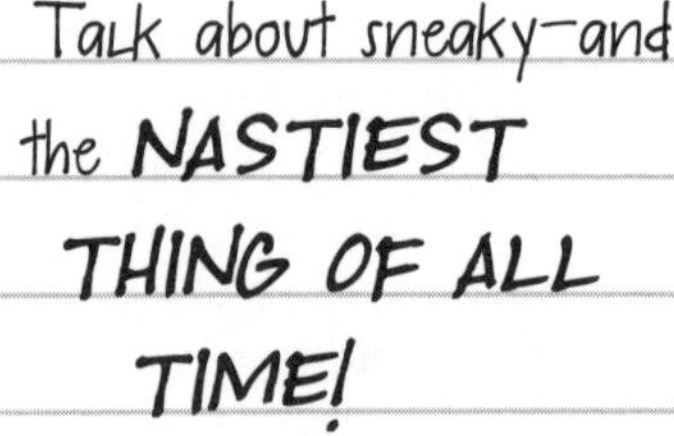

I'm sure Zoey thinks I have the craziest family in the universe.

AND SHE'S PROBABLY RIGHT.

At least Mom caught the Germ red-handed, or in this case, yellow-handed. "Jeremy Conrad, you need to learn to quit taking things that don't belong to you! I haven't forgotten that you ruined your sister's perfume, and now you've used poor Sophie's nail polish! No video games for three days. And don't start whining."

FINALLY!

I'm sure the Germ would have stomped, whined, and pouted if it hadn't been for Zoey standing there watching the whole thing go down. But instead, he just stood there with this weird look on his face when Mom handed down the punishment.

IT. WAS. PRICELESS!

Later Zoey said she might start coming to our A.C.E. meetings. Mom even volunteered to pick her up and said she could ride with us whenever she liked.

YES!

It was definitely one of the best spa nights in the history of spa nights.

Both Zoey and Sophie went home early last night since they have academic practice today. And get this: Miss Turner called and asked Mom if I'd like to help run the buzzer system at practice—and even participate in a few scrimmages. She probably asked because she felt sorry for me about the whole uniform thing. ☹

But who cares. I may not be smart enough to be on the team, but at least I can hang out with my friends and be a little useful.

I also have to go to church with Mom later and decorate the church for the baby shower. I can't believe the Campbells are finally coming home with their new baby tomorrow! Even better, that means we can hand a certain creepy creature back to Dylan! YES!!!!!!

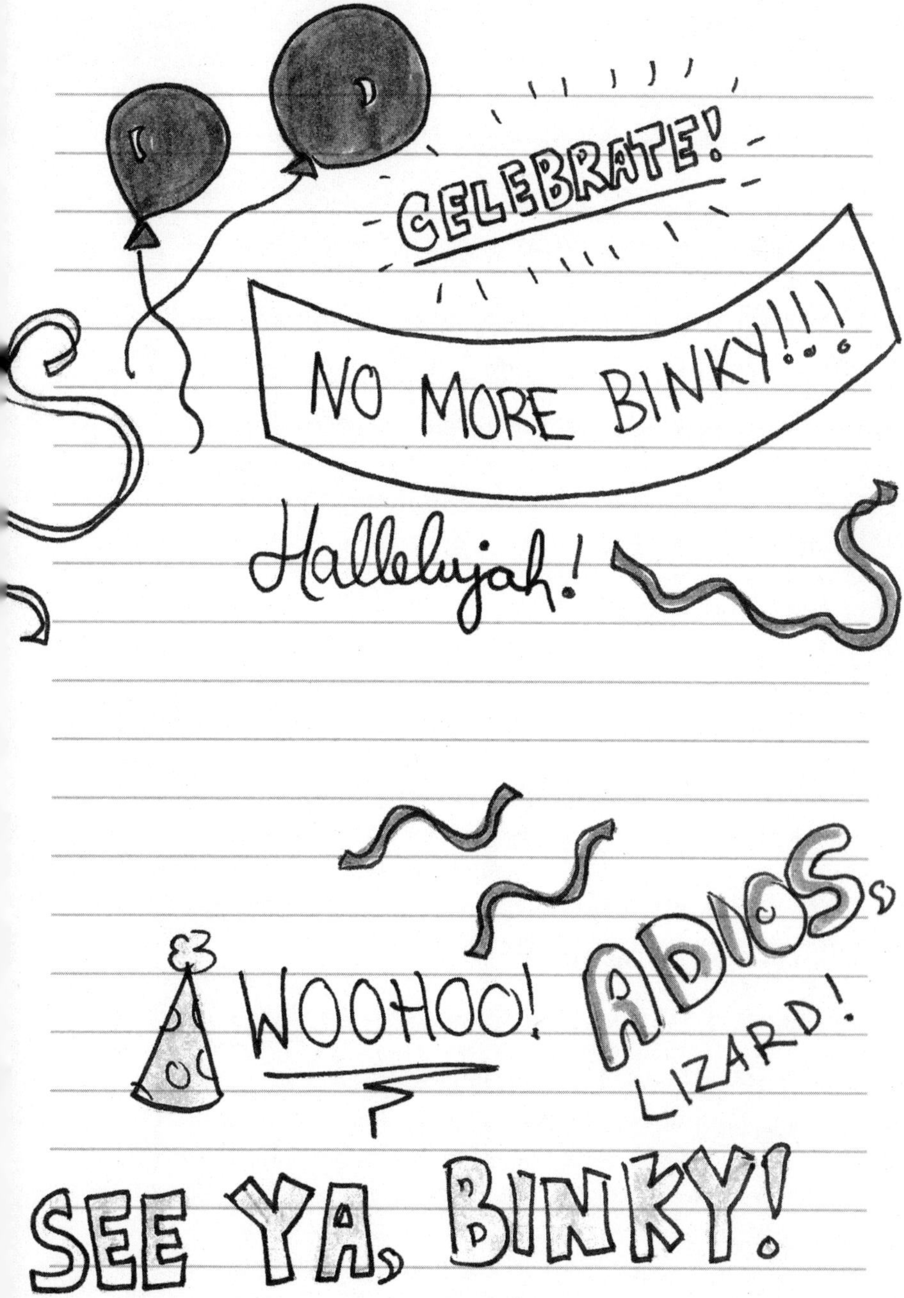

CELEBRATE!

NO MORE BINKY!!!

Hallelujah!

At academic practice, I could tell the entire team was nervous. But I don't blame them. The championship is just ONE week away, and they only have a few days to squeeze in some practice rounds. Ian started violin lessons a few months ago, and Lauren now has tennis a few days a week. Practicing every day is out of the question. Not only are my friends smart, they do all kinds of extra stuff too.

Not me.

I'm just an art kid. ☹

But when Miss Turner started asking questions at practice today, I couldn't believe it: I actually KNEW a lot of the answers!

I KNEW van Gogh painted Sunflowers!

I KNEW the capital of India was New Delhi!

I ***even KNEW*** the imperial palace in China is called the Forbidden City!

Miss Turner seemed just as shocked as I was.

But Sophie wasn't. "It's easy to see why you make such good grades in social studies, Catie. You're a BRAIN!" she said.

ME?

A BRAIN?????

Weird.

I've never been called THAT before. . . .

But I kinda liked it. ☺

SUPER BRAINIAC!

SUNDAY, FEBRUARY 9

I have waaaayyyyy too much to do today:

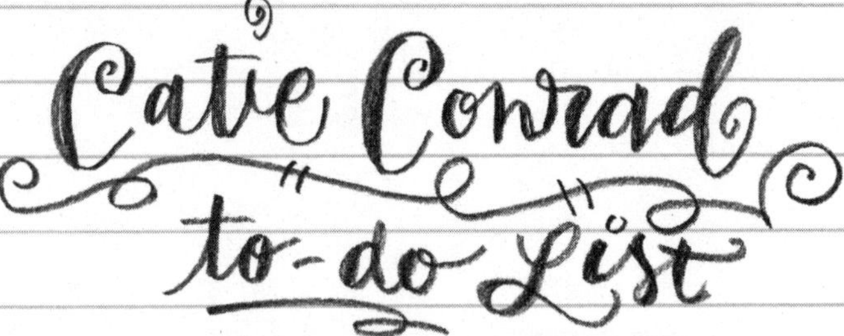

1. SUNDAY SCHOOL.
2. Meet Dylan & his family at the airport.
3. Go to the Baby Shower w/Mom.
4. Study for ART QUIZ!!

I thought Sundays were supposed to be a day of rest!

I also happen to be the ONE girl with the ONE brother who wakes everyone up at the crack of dawn. My chance of getting any rest with that kid in the house is **ZERO.**

He just now barged into my room, grabbed my measuring tape without asking, and ran back down the hall. I even heard him ask Mom for the blue duct tape from the craft box. Seriously, what is wrong with him?

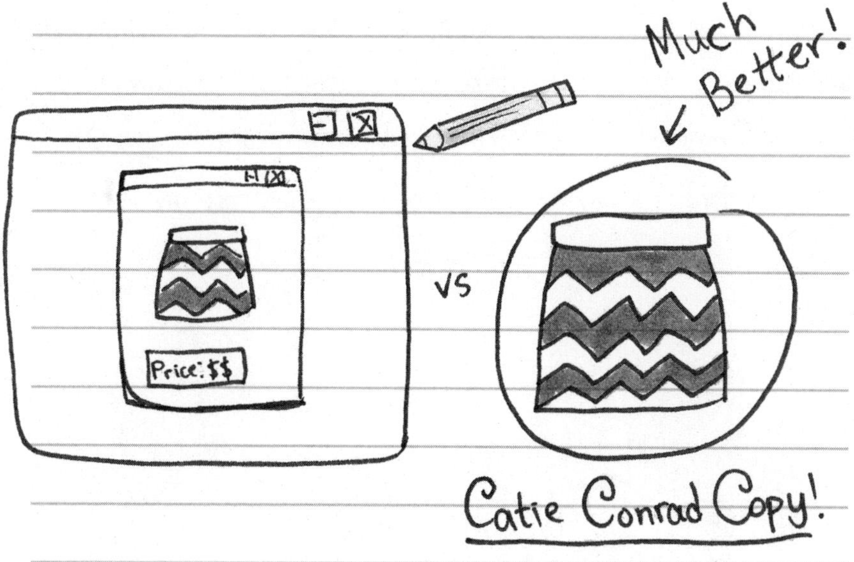

Who knows what he's up to now, but at least I have a little time to write in my diary and do a few fashion sketches.

I can't get this one skirt design out of my head. I'd seen one like it on the Internet a few days ago, but it's WAY too expensive. And since I'm giving Dad a little more of my allowance to send to Compassion International, I won't have the money anytime soon. Anyway, I think I can make one sort of like it, but WAY cheaper. ☺

If I can't design the uniforms for the academic team, at least I can make clothes for myself. I wanted to cut out the fabric last night but didn't have time.

We stayed at church until almost 9:00 P.M. putting up the baby shower decorations. The fellowship hall looks awesome, but my mouth still hurts from blowing up FIVE PACKS of pink balloons. Mom even let me decorate a few of the tables since she said I had great style. ☺

I wonder if J.H. will be at Sunday school today. . . . He rarely misses. Maybe he'll wear the dreamy blue striped shirt that he wore to school last week. He really could be a male model. ☺

I also noticed that he and Tyler have started putting stuff in their hair. Josh's always looks PERFECT, but I think Tyler overdoes it a little. I wouldn't dare say it to his face, but Tyler kinda looks like he uses that same Freeze It stuff that Sophie used on my hair Friday night.

That goop doesn't help either of us, if you ask me.

Gotta go! I suuuuuurrreeee hope Josh is there! I'm even wearing my blue-and-white floral dress today. It looks good with my eyes, AND I'll be the PERFECT MATCH FOR JOSH if he wears that shirt. ☺

Catie + Josh 4EVER

UGH.

Josh wasn't at Sunday school this morning.

Maybe he slept in?

So much for the extra time I spent trying to do one of those braids in my hair . . . Josh wasn't even there to notice me!

But I need to remember AGAIN what Pastor Steven says about trying to please others all the time. NOT GOOD.

It was also hard to concentrate on Mrs. Childers's lesson about Zacchaeus this morning. It made me think about my brother and that whole crazy tree thing. Even though the Germ isn't a tax collector like Zacchaeus, some people don't like him either. And even though he was hidden up in a tree, Zacchaeus wanted to see and know Jesus more than anything. THAT'S what mattered most!

GTG throw on some jeans and put the finishing touches on the welcome-home posters. Mom found my fluorescent markers from the science fair, and I'm going to outline the letters in neon green. They'll be so bright that Dylan's family will probably see them from the plane! LOL! LATER!

Outfit for the
Airport!
neon sleeves!
Matching neon
belt
-They won't be
able to miss us!

Okay, so I don't even know how to explain this. What I just witnessed may scar me for life.

I just discovered why the Germ stole my measuring tape last night.

OH. MY. GOODNESS.

My insane brother has really, really, REALLY lost it!

He made Binky a walking leash.

Yes, that's right. A LEASH FOR A LIZARD. He'd even made a little vest out of cardboard, covered it with blue duct tape, and wrapped it around Binky's stomach. Then he looped MY measuring tape through the vest and is using it as a leash!

"I saw one like it on the Love Your Lizard website," he said. "Even bearded dragons need exercise, so I decided to make one for Binky. See Catie, you're not the only one who can do fashion designs. At least my designs are USEFUL."

YOU HAVE GOT TO BE KIDDING ME!

There's NO WAY I'm getting in the car with Dad, my brother, and that leash-loving Binky. And riding ONE HOUR EACH WAY to and from the airport—with THEM?????

I don't think so.

NO WAY.

NO HOW.

NOT. IN. A. MILLION. YEARS. !!!!!!!!!!!

UGH.

I'm trapped in the car with Dad, the Germ, and that freaky lizard. ☹

Can Binky get out and walk around?
He needs his exercise.
UGH!

But at least I'm getting to sit up front since Mom is staying at church to get everything ready.

I'm writing in my diary to keep the GERM from irritating the living daylights out of me. At least Dad made him give me back my measuring tape. Dad rummaged around in the garage and found some string for him to use instead.

BUT. IT. STILL. LOOKS. HIDEOUS.

We hadn't been in the car ten minutes before we started arguing.

IRRITATED ME: You had BETTER have a tight hold on that leash! If Binky so much as TOUCHES the front seat of this car, you and that creature are BOTH gonna get it! I cannot wait for you to give that creepy thing back to Dylan!

IRRITATING GERM: QUIT calling him a creepy thing. I told you, his scientific name is **POGONA VITTICEPS**! If he

gets mad and puffs out his beard at you, don't blame him! It's YOUR fault!

MY BROTHER HAS OFFICIALLY LOST IT! He even asked Dad if we could stop at a rest area and let Binky stretch his legs a little. At least Dad told him no.

UGH.

THANK YOU, LORD!

Maybe if I doodle a little, I can block them out of my mind.

GTG! We're pulling into the airport! EEEEK!!!!!!! SOOO EXCITED!!!!!!!!!

WELCOME HOME LILY!

WELCOME BACK CAMPBELL FAMILY!!!

MONDAY, FEBRUARY 10

I only have a few minutes to write this morning, but OH. MY. GOODNESS. Lily is the cutest baby ever! She has black hair and the chubbiest little cheeks I've ever seen on a kid. The Campbells were totally surprised when they walked into the church fellowship hall and saw so many yell out "Congratulations!" Mrs. Campbell even let me hold Lily for a few minutes last night while she opened some of the gifts.

But they weren't the only ones surprised. Josh was there with his family too!

I should have expected it since Josh's mom always helps with special events at church. TALK ABOUT TENSION.

AND he looked as cute as ever, AND he was wearing that blue striped shirt, AND he smelled so good! Luckily, Sophie was there to make sure I didn't act like an idiot. The three of us just hung out at one of the tables and concentrated on eating the baby shower cake.

GTG!

I gotta pray about the art quiz before going to school. I didn't have much time to study last night and really need God's help on this one!

C YA!

NOW I KNOW WHY MONDAY IS THE WORST DAY OF THE WEEK.

I FLUNKED the art quiz. Yes, that's what I said—

I FAILED IT. ☹

So much for praying about things.

Mrs. Gibson had only ten questions on the quiz, so if anyone missed more than three, it was a *BIG FAT F*. It didn't take but two seconds for her to grade our papers and hand them back out to us.

I missed four, so that meant a 60% . . . F. ☹

At first I thought this might have been just a bad dream or something. But Mrs. Gibson snapped me into reality when she told us to get our books and correct the questions we'd missed.

I quickly turned my quiz face down so no one could see it. My heart started racing, and I felt sort of dizzy. And I had to bend over and get my pencil out of my book bag. After all, when you get light-headed, you're supposed to turn your head upside down, right?

But when I bent over, my paper flew off my desk, floated through the air, and slid DIRECTLY UNDER EMILY'S! ☹ It was like some weird puff of wind blew the paper right off my desk and into enemy territory. Emily reached down and looked at my paper, and her mouth dropped open big enough for a plane to land in.

UGH!!!!!!!!!!!!!!!!!!!!!!

"Here you go, Catie," she said. "I think this is yours, even though I CAN'T believe it."

EXTRA EXTRA!
CATIE CONRAD
FLUNKS ART
QUIZ!

I'm sure she passed a note to Miranda in two seconds and gave her the delightful news.

I wanted so badly to run out of the room. But I'd already used up one of my bathroom passes the last time Miranda upset me. I felt sick to my stomach, sorta like when Mom slips kale into our salads.

But that's not even the worst part of it: **MIRANDA GOT AN A.**

I can't even believe I'm writing this.

But it's true.

Miranda Maroni outdid me on an art quiz. And she didn't just outdo me—SHE GOT THE HIGHEST SCORE IN THE ENTIRE CLASS. ☹

Oh, and she had to make sure that EVERYONE knew about it. Especially me. *"Em, this is going to be the BEST week ever, don't you think?"* She squealed louder than a first grader. *"Valentine's Day is only four days away, AND I've started out the week by acing the big art quiz."*

UGH.

MIRANDA + THE NEW ART GENIUS + THE MOST POPULAR GIRL ON VALENTINE'S DAY = THE LUCKIEST GIRL EVER, and the WORST DAY EVER FOR ME. ☹☹

Mrs. Gibson probably could tell I was upset, but I didn't care. Sometimes she even asks me after class about my latest fashion project. But today *"the teacher who loves to flunk kids"* was the LAST person on earth I wanted to talk to.

Thank goodness the bell rang so I could dart to the bathroom and cry in private.

"So much for me being a brain, huh, Sophie?" I cried. *"I'm more like a total loser if I can't even pass a quiz on my best subject.*

I even prayed about this—just like I prayed about making the uniforms for the academic team. I don't think God hears a thing I say!"

But of course, Soph tried to make me feel better and put her arm around me. "I still think you're a brain, Catie," she said. "But maybe you should have just studied a little more, that's all. You did have a lot on your plate. And that doesn't mean God doesn't hear you, crazy girl. He knows what's best for you, more than you do."

There's one thing I'm sure of: getting an F on that quiz is NOT going to be what's best for me when Mom finds out. **I'll be grounded until I'm twenty.**

It was really all the Germ's fault. If he hadn't driven me bonkers with Binky this weekend, I could have concentrated on studying. Thank goodness that thing was back at Dylan's house. I never wanted to HEAR, SEE, or THINK about a bearded dragon for the rest of my life! Now if I could just figure out a way to get rid of Rosey.

Mom could tell I was a little depressed when I didn't even eat a second plate of fettuccine Alfredo tonight. I finally caved, gave her the bad news, and prepared for the worse. But Mom reacted WAY better than I expected. Of course, I got a lecture about organizing my time a little better. And about remembering that Mrs. Gibson did nothing wrong. She didn't fail me. I failed the quiz myself.

And even though taking my computer away for a week TOTALLY STUNK, it could have been worse—MUCH worse. She could have ended up scheduling a meeting with Mrs. Gibson, and then everyone in the WHOLE SCHOOL would know that CATIE CONRAD GOT AN F.

But I'm sure Miranda took care of that anyway.

At least I can go to my room and FINALLY get started on that new skirt design. Thankfully Mom didn't take away my sewing machine too. ☺ But just when I was getting ready to cut out the waistband, the phone rang, and Mom said it was Sophie.

SO WEIRD.

I wasn't used to talking to anyone on the phone—even Sophie. But since I don't have my computer and can't receive messages, my friends decided to use the old school method to make sure I was alive.

And that's when I received the **CRAZIEST, SCARIEST, MOST SHOCKING NEWS OF MY ENTIRE LIFE.**

Shocking Sophie: So I take it you told your Mom about the quiz, huh? Well at least you can still talk on the phone, otherwise I'd have to come over ASAP! You won't believe what just happened. **I AM SOOO UPSET.**

Confused Me: What's the matter? You're freaking me out a little. What happened? Tell me, already!

Even-More-Shocking Sophie: I stayed after school for academic practice today, and Zoey never showed up. **WE WAITED FOREVER.** Let me remind you that the regional championship is just FIVE days away. And get this: we found out that Zoey has mononucleosis—you know, **MONO.** It's sort of like the flu, but a zillion times WORSE.

Still-Confused Me: Wow, sorry Soph. That stinks. I sure hope she's okay. She'd better make a quick recovery.

Making-No-Sense Sophie: Get this—Zoey's mom told Miss Turner that there's no way she can compete this weekend. SHE'S OUT FOR THE SEASON. Can you believe it? I hope you don't mind, but I suggested to Miss Turner that maybe you could fill in for her. She'll probably ask you tomorrow.

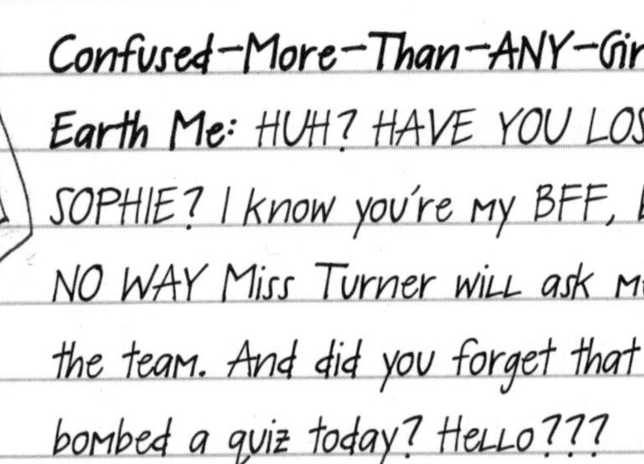

Confused-More-Than-ANY-Girl-on-Earth Me: HUH? HAVE YOU LOST IT, SOPHIE? I know you're my BFF, but there's NO WAY Miss Turner will ask me to be on the team. And did you forget that I just bombed a quiz today? HELLO???

Weirdly Calm Sophie: Okay, so you didn't do well on ONE quiz. BIG DEAL. That's what you reminded me when I stunk up Mrs. Bristow's social studies quiz—right? Pleeeezzzeee, Catie.

I wouldn't have suggested you to Miss Turner if I didn't think you could do it. Plus you've been to a lot of the practices so it's a NO-BRAINER. I'm hanging up before you try to say NO. C'ya tomorrow, BFF!

NO-BRAINER IS RIGHT. I feel like I have NO BRAIN when I'm around Sophie and all of her smart friends. And since I bombed the big art quiz, I feel like a failure around them AND Miranda Maroni. There's no way I can do this.

NO. WAY.

NOT. AT ALL.

PRAYER LIST MUST-DO'S

1. Thank God that Lily and her family are home safe and sound.
2. Pray that I make the right decision about this CRAZY idea of Sophie's.
3. Pray that I can accept when good things happen to Miranda and bad things happen to me.
4. Have FAITH.

.Faith.

TUESDAY, FEBRUARY 11

At least I was right about something.

Miranda knew all about me flunking the art quiz. She and Emily walked directly behind us on the way to science today—so close that I thought she was going to step onto the heel of my shoes. "Are you feeling okay today, Conrad? I know that yesterday sort of FLUNKED for you. . . . Oh, I mean STUNK."

She knew exactly what she was saying. "Just keep walking and ignore her," Sophie reminded me. "Just keep walking."

I wanted to turn around and let Miranda have it, but I couldn't even think.

WHY ARE THEY SO MEAN?

My brain was beginning to go blank anytime she was around. Just as we were going into Mr. Finkleman's room, we ran SMACK-DAB into Miss Turner. "Well, you're just the person I was looking for," she said. "I guess you've heard about poor Zoey.

But the team captain seems to think you're the best person for the job, and I have to agree with her. So can we count on you this weekend?"

It was just my luck that Miranda and Emily were right behind us and heard the ENTIRE conversation. And before I could even give Miss Turner an answer, Miranda snorted loud enough to wake the dead and laughed hysterically while she walked around us.

Oh, but Miss Bully wasn't done yet. She said to Emily, "Conrad on the academic team? That'll be the biggest mistake that team ever makes. I guess she DOES belong with a bunch of losers though."

And then Emily said back, "Yeah, they might as well forfeit the match before it even starts."

I couldn't believe Emily had the nerve to say that. Sometimes she actually seems normal and speaks to me and Sophie. But when she's around Miranda, she turns into a TOTALLY different person. Two-faced girls drive me CRAZY!

GRRRRR..............

But Miss Turner heard every word they'd said.

So had Mr. Finkleman. "I think it's time you two girls make a visit to see Principal Martin. Your rude behavior has gone far enough."

I. COULD. NOT. BELIEVE. IT!

JUSTICE!!!!!

I was so upset from all the drama that I couldn't think clearly or give Miss Turner an answer. I finally said, "Are you positive you want me on the team? You haven't talked to Mrs. Gibson recently, have you?"

I'm sure if they talked to one another in the teacher's lounge, Mrs. Gibson would have said, *"I'm not so sure about you asking Catie to be on the team. She failed my quiz and isn't a very good student."* Yeah, I'm sure it would have gone down like that.

But Miss Turner totally surprised me. "Yes, I'm sure about you being on the team. And in fact, I did speak with Mrs. Gibson, and she thought you'd be a wonderful choice too."

Whoa.

Seriously?

"I hope your decision isn't impacted by Miranda and Emily," she continued. "They're not acting appropriately, and I'm sorry you had to hear that. I have to run to class now, but you think it over and let me know tomorrow. I sure hope it's a yes!"

I could barely concentrate on a single thing in science class. What should I tell Miss Turner?

I had to snap out of it and concentrate.

Mr. Finkleman was teaching about bacteria and viruses and even explained why Zoey had to miss over a week of school. Apparently, since mono is caused by a virus, it can easily spread to the rest of us. YIKES.

Mr. Finkleman even said, "Mono is sometimes called the kissing disease, since it can be spread by saliva."

You should have heard everyone ooohing and aaahing and trying to figure out who Zoey had been kissing. But I knew she didn't have a crush on anyone, and I knew she wouldn't be doing that in the first place.

I AM shocked that Miranda doesn't have mono though. I'm sure she kisses LOTS of guys.

But Finkleman went on to say mono can also be spread by coughing, sneezing, or drinking after someone. Now I know why Mom always tells me not to drink after other people. Gross.

Suddenly, Matt blurted, "If you ask me, we all need to bathe in that anti-germ stuff from head to toe!"

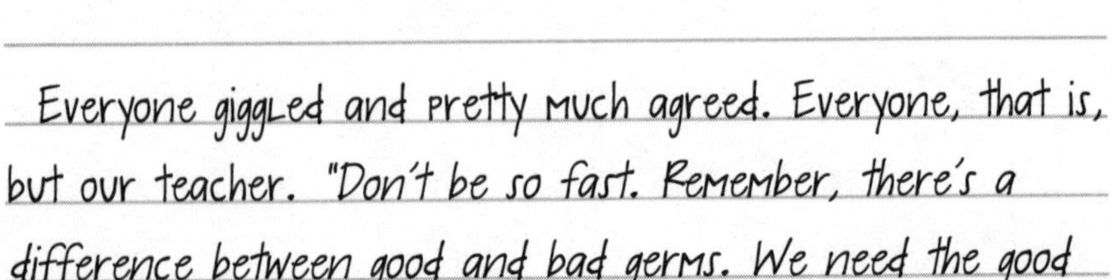

Everyone giggled and pretty much agreed. Everyone, that is, but our teacher. "Don't be so fast. Remember, there's a difference between good and bad germs. We need the good germs for a variety of reasons. For example, we need the good germs in our intestines to help digest food. I do believe it's perfect timing for everyone to complete this fun worksheet. Oh, and quiz tomorrow."

GRRRRR . . .

Everyone groaned and gave Matt a mean look. He just HAD to open his mouth and be the class comedian.

As I was reading about the different types of bacteria, Sophie got up to use the pencil sharpener and dropped a note onto my desk.

"PLEEASSEE SAY YES! WE NEED YOU! I ♥ YOU!"

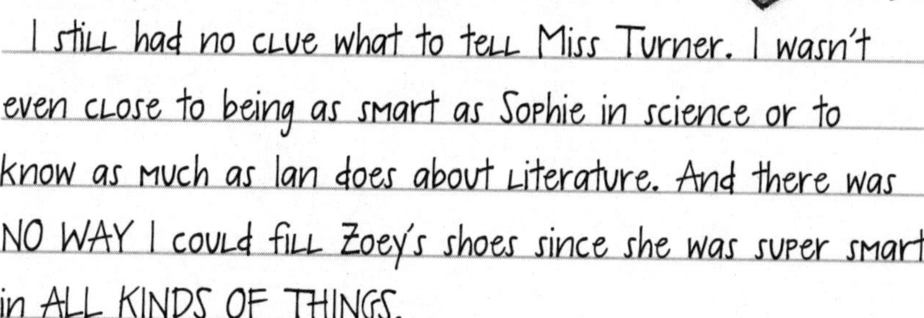

I still had no clue what to tell Miss Turner. I wasn't even close to being as smart as Sophie in science or to know as much as Ian does about literature. And there was NO WAY I could fill Zoey's shoes since she was super smart in ALL KINDS OF THINGS.

Surely they could find someone else.

But then something WEIRD happened. As Mr. Finkleman was walking through the aisles and checking our papers, he leaned over and said, "I think you should consider what Miss Turner is asking, Catie. Just because you're an artist doesn't mean you don't know about other things. Don't sell yourself short. Read about Leonardo da Vinci tonight. You'll see."

HUH?

What was the big deal about Leonardo da Vinci? First Mrs. Gibson talked about him in art last week, and now so was Mr. Finkleman.

STRANGE.

My science teacher was acting weirder than usual. I think he really believed in me.

Now if only I believed in ME.

WEDNESDAY, FEBRUARY 12

So . . . today's the day.

Not only do I have a HUGE science quiz (I actually studied for this one!) but I have to give Miss Turner an answer. The regional final is just THREE days away, and there are only two practices left. My brain hurts from thinking about it.

I still can't believe that she asked ME to fill in for ZOEY.

Unbelievable.

Of course, Sophie made it clear yesterday on what she thought I should do. And the fact that she called me THREE times about it last night made it crystal. I'm sure it was my BFF who put Ian and Lauren up to calling me on the home phone too.

I SOOOOO MISS MY COMPUTER!

Since this was such a big decision, I knew I needed to talk to Mom and Dad about it too. I needed all the help I could get.

"Sounds like a Moses opportunity if you ask me," Mom said.

Once again, my mother made no sense. Sometimes it's like she's FORCING me to THINK about something, instead of just telling me what to do already!

"I know the story of Moses," I told them. "But how on earth does that have anything to do with the academic team?" I don't recall him having to solve an algebra problem or answer science questions before a buzzer rang.

"Think about it," said Dad. "God chose Moses to do a really important job—to lead His people out of Egypt. Moses could have said, 'No, I don't think I'll do it.' In fact, Moses

even asked God to pick someone else. But God doesn't make mistakes. Perhaps you've been given this opportunity for a reason."

If only I felt as confident about this whole thing as Dad. I couldn't keep from thinking about bombing that art quiz or the fact that I had a C in science.

Why would Miss Turner want me?

"Moses even gave God one excuse after the other on why he couldn't do the job. But none of us are perfect," Mom said. "Even if you struggle a little in science, or perhaps should have studied more on that last quiz in Mrs. Gibson's class, God loves using people who feel inadequate. That's when God steps in and gives us strength—even when it's scary."

Wow. It was like Mom could read my mind!

I'd never thought about Moses like that before. Now I was even MORE confused—as if that was even possible!

I was so stressed that I didn't even work on my new skirt last night. I only lacked finishing the waistband, but I just wasn't in the mood. I'd also promised Dad that I'd start rearranging my priorities a little more:

GOD FIRST, SCHOOL SECOND, AND THEN FASHION DESIGNS.

I got out my Bible and read about Moses in the book of Exodus. I noticed the part where God provides Aaron, Moses's brother, to help him along the way.

I'm so glad God gave me Sophie to be my BFF and to encourage me about this whole academic team decision.

And speaking of brothers, even the Germ could sense something was wrong with me. He kept Rosey in her cage the entire evening and didn't bug me one single time.

Yeah, he could tell I was THAT upset. It's about time the Germ acted more like Aaron and gave me a little help! SHEESH!

Still . . . I had to make a decision. . . .

On one hand, it could be really cool . . . IF WE WON. I might actually BECOME POPULAR. The whole school already knows our academic team is one of the best in the region. (Well, everyone knows except Miranda and a few other jealous students.) And if we WON, my coolness factor would go through the roof!

It might even make up for the "uniform fashion fiasco."

That still bugged me more than I cared to admit—at least I can write in my diary how I really feel about it. ☺

But . . . what if we LOST? ☹☹☹

I'm sure it would be my fault somehow. What little popularity I had from being on the academic team would immediately go up in flames. ☹

Oh, and Miranda would remind me every single day that she was right—choosing me to be on the team was the biggest mistake Miss Turner ever made.

DEFINITELY NEED TO PRAY ABOUT THIS!!!

I also have to grab breakfast and find my red ballet flats—or as Miranda calls them, the clown shoes. And I gotta ask Mom if I can use her computer, even though I'm grounded. ☹ Mr. Finkleman asked me to read about Leonardo da Vinci, and I almost forgot.

It'll be just my luck that he'll ask me about it in class and I'll feel dumber than ever.

That's the LAST THING I need!!!

Later! School and THE DECISION await!

Well, I did it.

Drum roll please . . .

I told Miss Turner YES.

I've decided to do like Moses did, and GO!!

I am now an official MEMBER of the Clairemont Middle School academic team. ☺ ☺ ☺

I still think these uniforms are SAD, but I'm trying to remember it's what's on the inside that's most important.

I. AM. TRYING.

IT'S OFFICIAL!

When Sophie found out that I'd given Miss Turner my answer, she squeezed me so tightly that I almost passed out. And at this point, I needed air to get to my brain as much as possible since we have a TWO-HOUR practice right after school.

Even Josh came up to me at my locker and said, "Hey, I heard you're on the academic team now. Very cool. Congrats. I hope you guys win it all."

HE ACTUALLY SAID THAT TO ME! OH. MY. GOODNESS!!!

BUT OF COURSE, Miranda had to ruin everything.

As soon as she heard I was on the team, she cracked up and made sure I heard her: "Since when does Clairemont put art kids on their academic team? Especially ones who can't even pass an easy quiz. They must be desperate!"

Yes, she is that RUDE.

Apparently one trip to the principal's office isn't enough for girls like Miranda Maroni.

I wiped my eyes as quickly as possible so that no one could see me crying. How one girl could be that mean is BEYOND ME. But I tried to remember that God gives me strength—even when I'm dealing with Miranda. I also remembered how Emily had once let it slip to Sophie that ever since Miranda's dad had switched jobs, things hadn't gone so well at home for her.

But if you ask me, that is NO EXCUSE for her to be so cruel!

At least Mr. Finkleman was glad to hear of my decision to join the team. Besides what my parents had reminded me about Moses, the stuff I'd read about Leonardo da Vinci really made me think too. Da Vinci was a "polymath," which meant he was super talented in all kinds of things. He's famous for painting *Mona Lisa* and *The Last Supper*, but he also studied anatomy, physics, and even drew designs for parachutes and diving suits—hundreds of years before they even existed!

If one of the world's coolest artists EVER could do well in both science AND art, then maybe it's possible for me too—ESPECIALLY with God's help!

In fact, Finkleman's quiz didn't seem very hard today. I was even one of the first to finish.

Oh, but wait. . . . **WHAT IF THAT'S A BAD SIGN?**

What if I felt good about it when really I FLUNKED another one?

What if Miranda outdoes me again? MY LIFE WILL BE OVER!

ADD TO PRAYER LIST:

1. Thank God that I have such awesome parents who help me make good decisions.
2. Thank God that my teachers believe in me.
3. Try not to worry so much about EVERYTHING and trust in God MORE.

THURSDAY, FEBRUARY 13

I'm SO glad Pastor Steven talked about the importance of staying strong—ESPECIALLY when others tempt us to get angry or say things we shouldn't. Last night, he read **Ephesians 6:14–16:** "Stand, therefore, with truth like a belt around your waist, righteousness like armor on your chest, and your feet sandaled with readiness for the gospel of peace. In every situation take the shield of faith, and with it you will be able to extinguish all the flaming arrows of the evil one."

Miranda wasn't necessarily the evil one, but sometimes she sure acted like it. Let's hope today isn't one of them!

I also just realized that TOMORROW is Valentine's Day. ☹

I only remembered it after watching the Germ lick a zillion envelopes and run the ink out of my best pink marker last night. Why did he have to write his name so LARGE?

He could have saved ink if he'd printed GERM, instead of JEREMY. Two letters add up when you're sending Valentine cards to half the elementary school. GOOD GRIEF!

I'm soooo glad kids my age don't send out those immature little cards anymore. *Well, not out in public, that is.* If we want to send a card to anyone (I ALWAYS send a card to Sophie) then we usually slide it into the little vent in each other's locker. It's the next best thing to a real mailbox for kids our age. I plan on making my own Valentine cards tonight, to make it a little more personal.

That is, if I get time.

We only have two practices left—today and tomorrow, until the regional championship on Saturday. I won't have much time to write in my diary for the next few days because I have to STUDY, STUDY, STUDY.

SOOOOOO STRESSED!!!!!!!!!!

If Miranda starts up again at school today, I may go crazy! Oh, and if she outdid me on that science quiz, **I MAY GO BERSERK!!!**

Later. ☹

UGH.

I DREAD SCHOOL TODAY.

I should have known Miranda would act like a total angel today. After all, since Valentine's Day is tomorrow, she has to make sure to look like the SWEETEST, PRETTIEST, and most PERFECT girl on the planet.

WHAT. A. FAKE. ☹

She didn't have me and Sophie fooled for a second! Oh, but I'm sure some of the boys in class totally bought into it. Hopefully Josh wasn't one of them.

Why does everything seem to go Miranda's way?

But at least something cool happened to me: **I GOT AN A ON THE SCIENCE QUIZ! YES!**

At first I was almost positive that I'd flunked it. Mr. Finkleman looked over his glasses and DID NOT look happy. "I'm quite disappointed in these results," he said. "And since everyone is going to be learning what a bell curve is in the next chapter, I'll display the overall scores like this, before giving back your papers."

I just knew my grade was going to be on the FAR LEFT side—resulting in TOTAL CATASTROPHE. I'd probably lose my cell phone, my computer, AND even my sewing machine. ☹ I might as well go live in a cave.

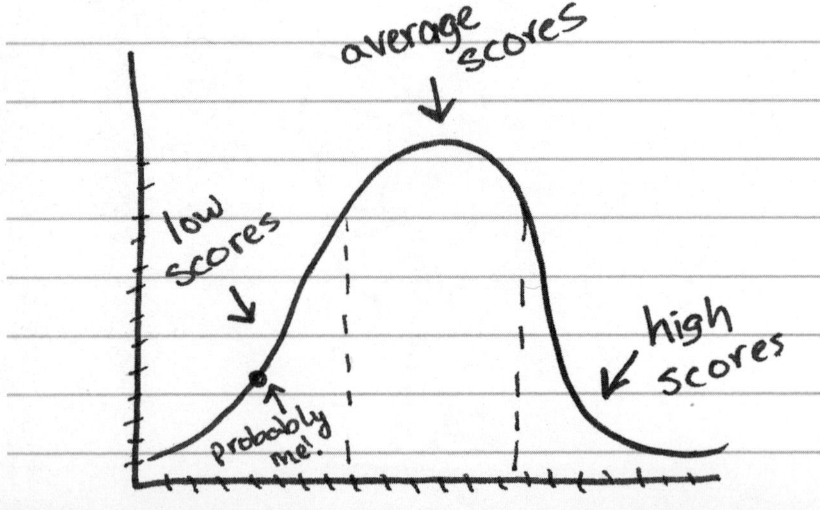

But after Finkleman placed my paper face down on my desk, I sloooooowly peeked under the corner.

It said 96% A!!

He even wrote "Nice work, Catie. Leonardo da Vinci would be proud. ☺" at the top. ☺

I glanced over at Miranda, hoping to tell by the expression on her face how she'd done on the quiz. But Miranda just kept smiling. She even looked RIGHT AT JOSH and SMILED. I'm almost sure I saw her wink at him, but I can't be sure.

UGH.

Gonna go reread Ephesians 6:14–16 again. I think I need it stamped into my brain so I can remember how to deal with the RUDEST and FAKIEST girl in school.

I can't believe what just happened!

EPHESIANS
6

Why didn't I think of this before?!

As I was rereading the verse in Ephesians, I got to the part that said "Stand . . . with truth . . . like a BELT AROUND YOUR WAIST," AND A CRAZY BUT BRILLIANT IDEA POPPED INTO MY HEAD:

BELT . . . DESIGN A BELT!

If I can't design uniforms for the team, at least I can make a belt for everyone to wear on Saturday! YES!!!

Gotta run!

← Simple & chic!

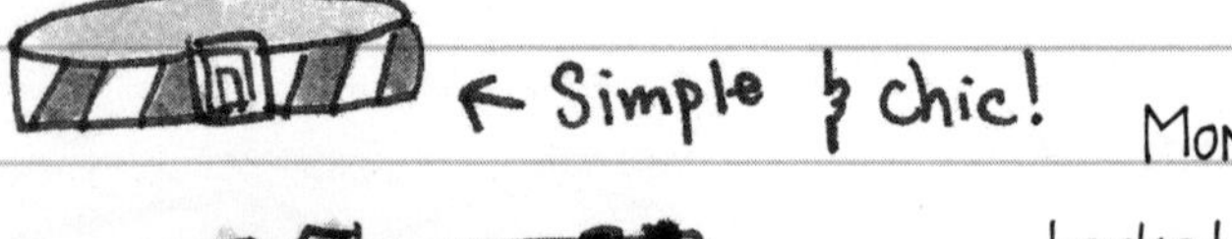

Mom just honked her horn, and I can't be late for academic practice!

I can't wait to tell Sophie about my belt idea. Of course, I'll have to ask Miss Turner if it's okay. ☺

↑ Silk belts are SO in!

I AM SOOOOO PUMPED!!!

FRIDAY, FEBRUARY 14: VALENTINE'S DAY ☹

Why does my life feel like one CRAZY roller-coaster ride that goes UPSIDE DOWN, BACKWARDS, and then all over AGAIN?

SHEESH! It was enough to make my stomach queasy 24/7. ☹

Don't get me wrong, yesterday's academic practice went GREAT. In fact, I can't believe I'm admitting this, but it was sort of fun trying to remember weird facts about stuff. It was even a relief to FINALLY learn how to work those algebra problems that hadn't made sense all year.

I was TOTALLY PUMPED when Miss Turner said I could go ahead and make belts for the team. I didn't even get upset when Ian said he'd rather have a tie than "a girly belt."

Totally doable.

I not only cut out all the fabric for the project last night, but I created Valentine cards for every member of the team. I even mailed one to Zoey, who was still not feeling well due to the mono thing. How I WISH I would have had the nerve to send Josh a card, but I didn't. ☹ My hand got sweaty just thinking about signing my name on something addressed to him.

HOWEVER . . .

When I got to school today . . . ***VALENTINE'S DAY*** . . . something happened that caused me to feel as sick as when I try to read in the car: Miranda hit the JACKPOT. ☹

From roses to chocolates to three, that's right, THREE stuffed animals—oh, and even a bottle of perfume—Miranda got everything she wanted. Some of the gifts were even from boys in eighth grade. ☹

And of course, she rubbed it in our faces.

She even had the NERVE to offer Sophie and me one of her chocolates! Yeah, she actually did that! Naturally we said, "No thanks," and tried to ignore her.

I couldn't wait to go to my locker and see if I'd received any Valentine cards. Since flowers or candy weren't happening, I hoped to at least score a few cards from my friends. I got nice ones from Lauren, Ian, Tyler, Matt, and several other kids in my class. Ian had even written in his card: "Thanks for the tie you're making me—I guess. LOL. ☺"

Sophie's card was awesome. She'd taped a few hairbands inside that said **"For Our Next Spa Night. Thanks for being the best BFF ever."**

I had one card left to open, but ran out of time and had to get to art class.

Mrs. Gibson passed out packs of those little heart candies that taste like stomach medicine and personalized cards she'd made for each of us. I suddenly felt horrible about being mad at her when I bombed the art quiz last week. She really cared about us, and I needed to remember that.

But then the **SICK** part of my day really happened.

OF COURSE, Emily just had to ask to smell Miranda's perfume, and OF COURSE, Miranda had to spray enough on her arms to stink up Mrs. Gibson's ENTIRE classroom.

YUCK!

I like the smell of gardenias, but it quickly smelled like a flower shop gone bad with a dead rat inside.

I suddenly craved fresh air. . . . My skin got clammy, my stomach gurgled, and I quickly asked Mrs. Gibson if I could get a drink of water. Sophie must have noticed I looked sick, too, since I heard her ask if she could go with me.

But before we even made it to the door, I. THREW. UP.

That's right. As **horrible** and **embarrassing** and **humiliating** as it sounds, I threw up all over Mrs. Gibson's floor.

I wanted to die, or at least vanish into thin air.

I overheard a bunch of the kids mutter "GROSS!" and a few of them start gagging like I'd made them sick too.

IT WAS AWFUL.

Mrs. Gibson hurried me to the bathroom and placed a wet cloth on my forehead. Sophie fanned me with a piece of paper. This was the **WORST** Valentine's Day EVER. There was NO WAY I was going back into that classroom—at least until next year.

Luckily Mrs. Gibson took me to the nurse's office and even allowed Sophie to stay with me. "I'm so sorry, Catie," Sophie said. "I was on the verge of hurling too. If Miranda thinks that perfume smells good, then she's crazier than what I thought. That stuff stinks worse than your brother's skunk."

After a few sips of lime soda, I started feeling better. I had to hurry and pull it together ASAP, since the school was having a pep rally for the academic team. I certainly didn't want to show up in the gym looking as green as an alien. Miranda would have LOVED THAT.

I'm so glad to FINALLY be home and have Valentine's Day O-V-E-R. But when I threw my book bag onto my bed, I realized I'd never opened the last card from my locker. I was sure it was from Miranda. It probably had a used piece of gum inside, or an anonymous note that said "LOSER." But when I tore into the envelope and slowly pulled out the card, I did a double take.

IT WAS FROM JOSH!!!!!!

It wasn't anything mushy or gross, just a standard card from the store. But at the bottom he'd written in his own handwriting,

"I'm **GLAD** we're friends. Happy Valentine's Day. Good luck tomorrow. Josh."

I couldn't help but notice he'd written GLAD in all CAPS!!!!!!

I gently placed the card in my purse, trying not to bend it, and could hardly wait to show Sophie at academic practice.

We both agreed that even if it didn't mean he had a crush on me, it obviously meant SOMETHING. Josh's card almost made up for my vomit nightmare at school today.

I immediately placed Josh's card in a secret place and started putting the finishing touches on the belts. THEY LOOKED AWESOME. And just as I was trimming Ian's tie, the Germ started beating on my door like it was some great emergency.

UGH.

I was hoping that the rest of my evening could actually be peaceful. I had plenty of studying and sewing to do, after all. But when I opened the door, I couldn't believe my eyes.

Brothers...

Gotta Love 'Em!

The Germ was standing at my door with a little vase holding three pink roses. "I hope you like them," he said. "I didn't want to send them to your class, 'cause I knew you'd get mad at me."

I. WAS. SPEECHLESS.

"If you hadn't told me how to deal with those boys at school, I'd probably still be asking Mom if I could stay home. Thanks for being the coolest sis ever," he said.

WOW. It was the nicest thing my brother had ever done for me. And the more I think about it, even if he HAD sent them to my class, I wouldn't have cared—even if it might make me look corny or unpopular.

My three little roses meant as much to me as the card from Josh.

Maybe even more.

Valentine's Day ended up being a success after all. I even let the Germ hang out in my room and quiz me on a few academic questions.

Now if I can just survive TOMORROW!!!!!!

ADD TO PRAYER LIST:

1. Pray that I don't embarrass myself and the team tomorrow!
2. Thank God for having a brother like Jeremy Conrad.

SATURDAY, FEBRUARY 15

GO TIME.

The regional championship match against Fayetteville Middle School starts at 11:00 A.M.

I can barely breathe.

I'm trying to remember what Mom and Dad said about Moses: God gave me this opportunity for a reason, and now I must try and help my friends.

I prayed again that I don't embarrass them and say something stupid.

Gotta get dressed, fix my hair, find some earrings, and pray that no one's belt falls apart!

Oh yeah, and then I gotta PRAY SOME MORE!

GTG!

EEEK!!!!!!!!!!!

Well, it's over! I can barely write in my diary because my hand is SHAKING!

I don't even know where to start!

First of all, JOSH and Tyler were there! I was afraid I'd pass out or throw up again, but I didn't. It's cool that even though they're on the basketball team and stay super busy, they came out and cheered on our team too. ☺

At the match, the questions the moderator asked were just as hard as Miss Turner told us they'd be. The score went back and forth the entire time, but I let Lauren, Sophie, and Ian buzz in and answer them.

I was too scared. I couldn't even put my thumb on the buzzer.

But when there was only one minute left, the coaches were allowed one time out to talk quickly with the team.

"Catie, you need to start buzzing in. I know you know some of these answers," Miss Turner said. *"Trust me, you can do this."*

Sophie told me the same thing. *"Come on and help us out, Catie. Snap out of it."*

I kept taking deep breaths and silently prayed that I could open my mouth and make words come out.

What if I gave the wrong answer?

What if I caused the team to lose?

What if I threw up in front of

But when I looked into the audience and saw my friends, my brother, Mom, Dad, and Mrs. Gibson and Mr. Finkleman, I suddenly felt a little better. Even Dylan and his family were there to cheer me on—Lily too!

"God called you to do this for a reason," I thought to myself. *"Remember Moses, for goodness sake!"*

But still, a tiny part of me wasn't so sure.

When the match resumed, the moderator started the clock and began asking more questions. *"On the color wheel, yellow is a primary color. What is the complementary color of yellow?"*

I KNEW THAT ONE! Complementary colors were on that art quiz I'd bombed. Luckily Mrs. Gibson had made us correct our answers.

I buzzed in and replied. **"Purple!"**

"That is correct," said the moderator. "Point goes to Clairemont."

EEEK!!! There were thirty seconds left.

I was still barely breathing.

We were now only one point behind Fayetteville, 21–22.

"What is the symbol for sodium chloride, more commonly known as salt?" asked the moderator.

Darn it! If only I'd paid more attention when Finkleman went over that stuff.

"NaCl," Sophie quickly buzzed in and answered.

"That is correct," said the moderator. "Point to Clairemont. The score is now tied."

10 SECONDS LEFT!

DOUBLE EEEEEEEEK!!!

Ten seconds left. Score: 22–22.

My heart was about to explode out of my chest. Suddenly all of the stuff I'd studied started swirling around and getting mixed up in my head.

Why in the world did I EVER think I could actually be a popular brainiac kid like Sophie and the others?

I'm an art kid. It's just that simple.

The moderator had one question left.

"Reptiles often have defense mechanisms that protect them in the wild. Chameleons, for example, change colors. What reptile has the ability to puff out the scales around its neck whenever it feels threatened?"

You've GOT to be kidding ME!

I slammed that buzzer and replied, **"Bearded dragon!"** just a second before Fayetteville.

"*That is correct,*" the moderator said. "*Final point to Clairemont. Congratulations to the new regional champions!*"

Everyone jumped out of their seats and attacked me with hugs. Mom and Dad were even crying. LOL.

Josh and Tyler came over and gave everyone double high fives, and I turned ten shades of pink again.

Miss Turner made the team line up and get photos made for the town newspaper, and Principal Martin commented that the accessories I'd created looked nice with the uniforms. He even asked if I'd give my opinion about next year's uniforms, when we had more time. Ian said he might even wear his tie to school on Monday. ☺

Regional Champs!!!

Of course, my brother had to squeal at the top of his lungs, "SEE? I told you bearded dragons are cool! SEE? Maybe now Mom and Dad will buy ME one!"

UGH!

So typical of my brother. But I need to be a little more patient with him.

After all, not all GERMS are bad. ☺